"I don't even remember my own name."

His mouth was so close, so tempting. His face carried an evening shadow that only served to reinforce her earlier reaction to his masculinity.

The feeling of warmth spread through her body like a wildfire fanned by the wind, causing her breasts to swell and her breath to become shallow. She couldn't help but stare at his lips: so masculine, so inviting.

He slowly lowered his head, bringing his lips only inches from hers. A little warning bell sounded in her head, reminding her that she was about to start something she wasn't sure if she was ready for.

And if she crossed that line, there was no going back.

While he was her husband, she still didn't know him. She didn't know what their relationship had been like before the accident.

She clenched her hands into fists, determined not to place them against his chest, stand up on her tiptoes and press her lips to his.

* * *

Stranger in His Bed is part of the Masters of Texas series from Lauren Canan!

Dear Reader,

Welcome to the third book in the Masters of Texas series, *Stranger in His Bed*.

Wade Masters returns home after receiving word that his wife has been in a potentially life-threatening accident. Arriving at the hospital, he finds her battered and bruised, but the overshadowing concern is amnesia. The doctors can't say if it's permanent or temporary.

Victoria Masters knows nothing about the handsome man standing next to the bed. She doesn't remember his mansion home or anything about her life up to this point. She can't remember their shared passion or the touch of his lips on hers. Worst of all, it seems he wants nothing to do with her. She becomes determined to triumph over whatever came between them.

As the weeks pass, while her memories remain locked away, her love for Wade grows. When he confesses theirs is only a marriage of convenience, she is taken aback but determined to make the elusive billionaire fall in love with her. When he takes her into his arms and makes her his, their future is set.

Or is it?

Is there more to their passionate story? Can either withstand the shocking truth when her memory returns?

Lauren

LAUREN CANAN

———

STRANGER IN HIS BED

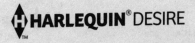
HARLEQUIN® DESIRE

Recycling programs
for this product may
not exist in your area.

ISBN-13: 978-1-335-97173-9

Stranger in His Bed

Copyright © 2018 by Sarah Cannon

Printed in U.S.A.

When **Lauren Canan** began writing, stories of romance and unbridled passion flowed through her fingers onto the page. Today she is a multi-award-winning author, including the prestigious Romance Writers of America Golden Heart® Award. She lives in Texas with her own real-life hero, two crazy dogs and a mouthy parrot named Bird. Find her on Facebook or visit her website, laurencanan.com.

Books by Lauren Canan

Harlequin Desire

Terms of a Texas Marriage
Lone Star Baby Bombshell

The Masters of Texas

Redeeming the Billionaire SEAL
One Night with the Texan
Stranger in His Bed

Visit her Author Profile page at Harlequin.com, or laurencanan.com, for more titles.

This book is dedicated to Terry:
the one who keeps me going. I couldn't write
without your inspiration and encouragement.

And to Kathy Douglass,
the best critique partner you could ever hope for.
Thank you for all you've done for me!

And many thanks to my editor,
Charles Griemsman. Bless you for your brilliant
guidance and for having the patience of a saint.

One

"I think she's awake."

As her vision cleared, the most beautiful pair of eyes she'd ever seen came into focus. They were a vibrant brown with so many flecks of gold they appeared to gleam. Framed by dark lashes, they were strong, compelling, and she couldn't look away. She didn't want to look away. It was as though they offered a lifeline and she desperately held on.

Her gaze widened to take in the rest of this man's face. The sharp angles and high cheekbones. The full, sensuous lips, drawn into a straight line, surrounded by a dark bearded shadow. His thick, tobacco-brown hair gleamed golden where the fluorescent lights touched it.

A second man in a white lab coat stepped into her field of vision on the opposite side of the bed.

"I'm Dr. Meadows, your neurologist." He spoke softly, clearly. Something she was grateful for.

The glaring white lights overhead burned with the same intensity as the sun. The pounding in her head became more pronounced, almost overwhelming, throbbing in time with her heartbeat.

"You were involved in an automobile accident two days ago. You had some injuries. Most were minor, but you did sustain a fairly bad concussion."

The doctor withdrew a pencil-sized flashlight from the pocket of his lab coat and pointed the light quickly into one eye, then the other. She couldn't help flinching as the beam touched her eyes. He returned the light to his pocket and flipped open a chart. After sifting through an array of pastel-colored pages, he made a notation on one of them before closing the folder.

"Can you tell me your name?"

"I'm… My name is…" She drew a blank. *How can I not know my own name? How is it possible?* Confusion added to her pain. "I don't know," she whispered almost to herself. A feeling of panic slowly crept in.

"Do you know who that man is?" The doctor nodded toward the stranger.

Once again she took in his features, the solemn face that was so full of character, the deep jaw and those eyes, so mesmerizing. But nothing about him was at all familiar.

"No." She slowly rolled her head against the pillow. "Should I?"

"I'm Wade," the man said, his deep voice conveying strength. "Wade Masters. I'm your husband."

Husband? She was married? The stunned disbelief must have shown in her eyes, because Wade Masters's expression turned into a frown of serious contemplation, and his eyes snapped across to the doctor. No. That couldn't be right. Could it? She raised a hand to her forehead. Frantically she searched her mind for any memory of a wedding. Of him. Of them. Of their life together.

Nothing.

"I don't know you." She heard the emotional quiver in her own voice. "I'm not married. How can you say that?"

Alarm set in, adding to the pounding in her head. This was all wrong. They had the wrong person. They thought she was someone else. She had to get up. She had to leave. She had to go home. Grabbing the railing at the side of the bed, she tried to pull herself into a sitting position. Hands immediately pushed her gently back down onto the pillow. "No. Please. I need to go home. I need to call…" *Who? Who was she going to call?* She couldn't think. Her head hurt. Everything hurt, and she had no memory of the person she was or the life she had known.

She heard the doctor call for a nurse. "Try to relax, Mrs. Masters," he said. "You're going to be fine. Your home is waiting when you regain your strength. You took a pretty hard knock on the head. Try not to worry if you can't remember people or names, including your own. With this type of injury, retrograde amnesia is not at all uncommon. I'm confident everything will come back to you in time."

"When?" She felt a tear slip down the side of her face. "When will it come back?"

"Unfortunately, we have no way of knowing how any one individual will react. Occasionally a memory may come to you as a kind of flashback. Then you may start to remember everything all at once, or it may come back in small fragments, like random pieces of a jigsaw puzzle. It could return tomorrow or months from now."

Months? No. She had to remember. There was something important she had to do. People were counting on her. She sensed a need to hurry. But the more she tried to recall the circumstances, the harder the hammer slammed into her head.

"Your tests have come back and everything is looking very good." The neurologist continued flipping through forms in her chart. "The cerebral swelling is all but gone. Your heart sounds good. Blood pressure is within a normal range. If no other concerns surface, we can talk about sending you home tomorrow." He looked from the chart directly to her.

A nurse bustled in. She injected medication into the intravenous tubing. "This should take effect in just a few minutes. I'll be back to check on you, sweetie." She nodded at the two men and left the room as quickly as she'd come in.

As I mentioned to your husband," the doctor said,

"there is a good chance being in familiar surroundings will stimulate the return of your memory."

Her husband. She returned her gaze to the tall man with broad shoulders who stood to her left, watching her in silent consideration. He was dressed in a dark business suit, his blue-and-gold-striped tie loosened at the neck, the top button of his white dress shirt undone. Her gaze fell on his hands, which were resting on the metal bar of the bed. They looked strong and capable. A gold wedding band gleamed on the third finger of his left hand.

She swallowed back the fear that something was terribly wrong.

"We will get through this. You're going to be okay." The man leaned down, bringing his face closer to hers. His hand covered her own, and the warmth felt good. His voice was as deep and seductive as his eyes were mesmerizing. "If there is anything you need…"

"Please tell me who I am."

"Your name is Victoria. Victoria Masters."

The man stood up straight, appearing relaxed and self-assured, and slipped his hands into the pockets of his trousers. She realized her initial impression that he was attractive had been an understatement.

He was *devastatingly* attractive.

She could smell his rich, enticing cologne. His white shirt set off his tan skin. The sharp lines of his face and the straight, proud nose were indicative of good breeding. His hair with its slight wave hung just past his collar and shadowed his forehead. The golden intensity of his eyes and the lack of a smile on those full, sensuous lips brought it all together: Wade Masters was the personification of danger. Not dangerous like a criminal, but dangerous like a man who was capable of stirring a woman's passion with little to no effort. And he knew it. It was part of that confidence he emitted.

And he was here to take her home.

With his gaze trained on her, she felt a heated blush rush up her neck and over her face. The barest hint of a smile touched his lips as though he knew what she was thinking. She looked away, swallowing hard.

The doctor interrupted her thoughts. "Right now, I don't want you to worry about memory recall. Try to relax and give it some time."

She felt the drug the nurse had given start to take effect and her eyelids grew heavy. She fought to keep them open, wanting to know more about the man who claimed to be her husband.

Dr. Meadows turned toward him. "I want to see her in two weeks. Have someone contact my office and set up an appointment. If she develops any dizziness, vomiting or severe headaches, bring her back to the ER immediately." He looked at his patient. "Bed rest for a day, then you can move around, but go slowly. No hundred-meter hurdles for at least a week." He winked at her, then smiled.

"Okay." She couldn't help but return his smile.

"You folks have a good day." He handed Wade his card. "If you should have any questions, don't hesitate to call."

"Thank you, Dr. Meadows," she said as the good

doctor disappeared out the door and down the hall. Her gaze returned to the other man. She felt a wave of anxiety shimmy down her spine. She was alone with this person, this man who claimed to be her husband. She still didn't recognize anything about him. There was nothing in his voice or the way he moved that was remotely familiar. For all his sex appeal, he seemed cold, unfeeling. Would she have married a man like that? Apparently so. Surely there was something about him or about their situation that would register?

There were so many questions she wanted to ask. She felt as though she was standing on the edge of a precipice, about to plunge down into the dark depths of the unknown. Could she do this? Evidently there was only one way to find out.

He had not made any other move to touch her. No hug. No kiss—even on the cheek. In fact, she'd received more compassion from the doctor and nurse than from the man who said he was her husband. Maybe he was just holding back because he knew she had no recollection of him? If that was the case, she appreciated his thoughtfulness. If not, they obviously had a major problem within their marriage and one she could do nothing about until her memory returned. She hoped, yet again, that would happen soon. In the meantime, she had to speculate about what would be asked of her. What would her husband expect?

The pain in her head and body began to fade, and before she could ask another question, she returned to the comfort of oblivion.

* * *

Wade Masters stood motionless as he watched Victoria fall back to sleep. She'd been monitored closely for the swelling in her brain and tested often to ensure no veins in her head ruptured from the building pressure. Today, when he'd received the call that she seemed to be regaining consciousness, he'd come to the hospital immediately. This, after having to cut short a business trip to London when he'd first heard of the accident.

He hadn't been prepared for the news of her amnesia. Or the fear he'd seen in her eyes, the way her gaze had held his as though his strength was the only thing holding her together. She'd looked at him with desperation and a silent cry for help, and he'd not been able to stop himself from wanting to make everything better. It had to be tough to wake up in a hospital and not remember your own name or what happened to put you there.

He was equally surprised the snobbishness she normally wore like a shield was gone. She tended to walk a fine line between arrogant and outright rude. But instead of demanding answers from the doctor, she'd asked questions with true concern and a hint of anguish in her voice. Still, she might not have the strength to be demanding. Perhaps it was all the pain and medication. Whatever the cause, something had changed. It was more than the cracked ribs and head injury. He had come here anticipating the worst, expecting he would have to deal with her demanding behavior. Instead, he encountered a woman who was frightened and wasn't afraid to let that anxiety show.

And the way she appeared now, without a half ton of makeup covering her face and her hair in disarray, she looked amenable and, in a strange way, actually more attractive than usual. Despite the bruising from the accident, she was a very beautiful woman.

But she was fastidious about the way she looked. The hospital staff had better keep any mirrors well away from her until she healed or be prepared to bear her wrath and interminable temper. They all had better relish this peaceful time. The true Victoria would be back soon enough.

It was too bad, because she had so much to offer. If only she would get a grip, stop being so superficial and entitled, and set goals for her future.

With one last glance at the woman sleeping in the bed, he grabbed his briefcase from the chair and walked out into the corridor. As he approached the row of elevators, his mind was spinning. He had to get a handle on how to deal with this. Maybe Dave Renner, his attorney, could shed some light on what the hell he should do now. The documents to end this sham marriage had been prepared and were awaiting Victoria's signature. They had both agreed to a settlement offer. In a matter of days he would have been free of her and all the baggage that came with her, including the outrageously snooty and often flamboyant behavior.

He would have been free of this woman who was his wife in name only.

His jaw clenched in frustration. He knew there was no easy answer. In fact, there was only one answer.

Take her home when she was released and care for her until she completely recovered. He shook his head at the unbelievable twist of fate.

Wade was glad Victoria would eventually be okay. He certainly wished her no ill will. He'd had his secretary clear his calendar for the next few weeks so he could remain close until she was better. Anything she needed would be provided. But he couldn't help but speculate if she would keep the amnesia thing going even if her memory returned. Her ability to maintain a lie was one of her best attributes. It was why he'd chosen her.

He pressed the elevator call button, still grinding his teeth. Their arrangement had been intended to benefit them both, giving her a much-sought entry into Dallas's inner circles and providing him with the facade of being a settled family man, which worked to his advantage in business negotiations. It had also been intended to eliminate unwanted emotions and potential complications found in a real marriage, something he had neither the time nor the patience to deal with. Those complications had been replaced by new ones, but at least it had provided him the freedom to come and go as he deemed necessary, and of late *go* seemed the option that worked best. The less time he spent in her company, the better.

Eight months after signing the agreement that bound him to her as her husband, she'd begun to be seen with various men out in public, often making the gossip columns, effectively negating the very purpose for which he'd needed her, causing all the carefully staged efforts to blow up in his face. After she'd ignored repeated requests for discretion, her actions had continued, albeit on a lesser scale, but enough that he was still not happy, especially when it had begun to negatively affect his business dealings and made him appear the fool, which he would not permit. Victoria had scoffed and asked him if he really expected her to live like a nun. He'd assured her that was not his intention. What he did demand was discretion. He'd reminded her of her desire for social esteem and warned she was about to lose all she'd set out to achieve. She'd ignored him, deciding to call his bluff. Other measures had to be taken. He had thought she was intelligent enough to know he would not allow this to go on, and she had pushed him as far as he would tolerate. The bottom line: she was an employee paid to act the part of his wife, and had been compensated very well for that effort. In addition, if she had lived up to the terms, she would have received a million-dollar settlement at the end of a year. Now less than a week away from being free of her, she'd had this accident.

He drew in a breath and blew it out as the doors to the elevator opened. He was stuck with an impetuous, ill-tempered wife in name only, who would most likely milk this amnesia thing for all it was worth. He fought to control his temper.

He needed to call his brothers Cole and Chance, who resided in Calico Springs on the Masters family compound. He hadn't spoken to either of them since his flight had landed. He supposed he should call Victoria's mother, too, to tell her she'd be out of the hospital soon. But all Corrine was really worried about was herself and ensuring her rank at the top of the social food chain lasted a while longer. And really, wasn't that all that mattered? He scoffed at the woman's preposterous behavior. If one of his brothers had been injured, he would not have stayed home and requested a daily update. He would be there at the hospital, not waiting for a phone call. His brothers would do the same. They showed up for each other. He almost felt sorry for Victoria. After being raised by that woman, it was no wonder she acted the way she did.

Bracing himself, he speed-dialed Corrine's number and headed for the side entrance door of the hospital, where his car and driver waited.

Two

As the doctor had promised, a nurse arrived at her room with a wheelchair the next afternoon. Victoria had requested that the flowers she'd received be given to other patients who might not have family. She didn't recognize the names on any of the cards anyway. Her clothing had been discarded when she had been first brought into the ER. Her husband had arranged for some loungewear to be delivered.

They headed toward the front entrance, the nurse pushing the wheelchair, Wade following. As they cleared the automatic glass doors to the outside, she embraced the warm afternoon air and the sounds of normal life all around her. It was summer, the trees were green and plants in full bloom, the colors so bold it was hard to take it all in.

What had she been doing before the accident? Where had she been going when she was hit? She turned her gaze from the flowers to focus on where they were headed now. Directly in front of her was a champagne-colored stretch limo waiting in the circular drive.

"Oh, my gosh," she uttered in complete surprise when two men stepped out. A driver and a *bodyguard*? One came around the car to open the rear passenger door for her. She looked up at her husband. "Is this yours?"

"It is."

"Seriously? I don't think I've ever been in a limo before. Maybe at a funeral…"

Wade smiled. "Actually, you have ridden in a limousine many times, but, since you don't remember, let's hope you enjoy this ride like it's your first. And we will certainly steer clear of any cemeteries."

He placed his hand under her arm and gently helped her stand and take three steps to the limo. Once inside, she leaned back against the rich leather seat and inhaled the new-car scent. Closing the door, Wade walked to the other side and got in next to her. Seconds later, they were off.

The scent of his cologne, distinctly masculine with hints of spices and sandalwood, blended with the rich smell of the leather upholstery. It was a heady aroma.

"Do you need the temperature adjusted?" he asked. "Are you comfortable?"

"I'm fine. It feels strange to be outside again. Good. But strange."

He nodded as though he understood.

"We're near Dallas, aren't we?"

"Yes. You remember Dallas?"

She pointed at the window to his left. "I recognize the skyline."

He nodded.

"How long have we known each other? Where did we meet?"

He seemed to hesitate, looking out the window before turning to face her. "We met at a party. Several years ago."

She again let her eyes fall on this man who was positively dripping in sex appeal. It seemed too much to accept he was her husband. He fell into the category of something too good to be true. And didn't that usually turn out to be right? But she would run with it while it lasted. Until her memory returned, there was little else she could do.

"Let me guess," she said with a smile. "You saw me from across the room and couldn't take your eyes off me. It was love at first sight, right?"

He appeared amused. Amused was good. Better than the deadpan stare that was all she'd seen so far.

"You made…an unforgettable impression. As you are now."

That shot the nurse had given her this morning must have been the cause of her runaway mouth. She wanted to giggle for no apparent reason. But maybe that was normal in her circumstances? She took a deep breath and tried for sincerity.

"How long have we been married?"

"Almost eight months."

"Practically newlyweds. Maybe that's why I can't remember you."

"Possibly, but not likely."

She had to agree. Short of an injury like hers, how could she ever forget loving and being loved by a man like Wade Masters? "What do you do? Like, for a living?"

"I have a business. Actually, it's a family business."

"Let me guess." She gave a tiny snort. "You make pizza, and this is the delivery van?"

Again those eyebrows shot up, and the tiny smile returned.

"Close. Avionics, electronics, ranching, Masco Laboratories… I'm sure there must be a Domino's Pizza in there somewhere." The gleam was back in his eyes as he tilted his head. "Are you hungry?"

"Yes. No. Depends on what you've got."

Again he turned toward her, giving her a look of surprise. She hadn't meant it the way he might have taken it, but she couldn't stop the blush that crawled up her neck. She was hungry, all right. Hungry for knowledge; starving for memories, good or bad. And if he didn't curb that sexy hint of a smile, she would be well on her way to hungry for him. Who was this guy? How in the hell had she met and married a man like Wade Masters? It didn't feel right. But at the moment it didn't feel all that wrong.

"There will be a wide selection when we arrive at the house. You can eat at your leisure." His voice rolled over her, deep and solemn as he readjusted in his seat. "I'm certain we can meet any needs you might have."

"Anything?"

He smiled a wide, unpretentious smile. "I'm fairly certain we can keep you well satisfied."

What needs would she have? More important, what needs would *he* have, and what expectations would he have of her? She could see him pulling her into his arms and carrying her to a large bed in a master suite for a night of... *Oh, God.* Moaning softly, she closed her eyes and rubbed her forehead. What was it about this guy that made her thoughts run straight to the gutter? One quick sideways glance and she saw him smirking. Did he read minds? At least he had a sense of humor. While she couldn't explain it, she couldn't see herself marrying someone who didn't. That was the most important thing. It was what got you through everything else in life.

Gathering herself, she raised her chin and straightened her shoulders. "Do I have any brothers or sisters?" *A safe topic.*

"No. As far as I know, only your mother and father." He pulled a cell from his inner suit pocket, glanced at the screen, then put it back. "I have spoken to Corinne daily since the accident. I'm sure she would like to hear your voice. You might want to give her a call."

"Corinne? Is that my mother's name?"

"It is."

"Sounds like some sort of bleach."

Wade ran a hand over his mouth and jaw as though he didn't know what to make of that one.

A mother. And a father. Add two more people to the list of folks she just didn't remember.

A memory suddenly surged through her mind accompanied by dull pain. She was standing just outside the front door of a redbrick house, a blonde woman hugging her. They were both crying. But it didn't feel like it was her mother.

This memory loss was absolutely the worst thing she'd ever been through. At least that she could remember. The other injuries from the collision took a back seat by comparison.

The rest of the drive passed in quiet contemplation. Who was Wade Masters? Where were they going? She didn't sense anything sinister about him except maybe a wicked sense of humor. In spite of him being well above normal in the looks department, he was well mannered and courteous, not snobbish, at least not that she'd picked up on. Granted, she'd seen him only two times—that she could recall—but, while he was apparently wealthy, he didn't give the impression he held himself in higher esteem than anyone else. Neither did he seem like a happily married man. She would have expected him to hold her, kiss her or give reassurances. *Something.* But he remained aloof. Polite to a fault, but distant.

Eventually the limo turned into a driveway, coming to a stop in front of tall black wrought-iron gates. They opened immediately and the car proceeded up the hill and to the right where a circular drive dipped under a high portico. She had a strong suspicion it was the largest house she'd ever seen. A mansion complete with turrets that made it look more like a castle than a house.

"Is this where you live?" The sheer colossal size of it required confirmation.

He nodded as the driver opened his door. "This is where *we* live."

She leaned toward the window and glanced up at the top of one of the towers, then back to her husband. "I guess the ghosts don't come out until night."

He looked at her with surprise. One eyebrow lifted higher than the other, and then he once again pursed his lips as though hiding a smile. "I guarantee it. And if you become frightened, I'll be close by."

She didn't think she was a negative person, but if the good doctor hoped coming to live in this place was going to stir any memories, he was sadly mistaken. She might not remember a ride in a limo, but no way would she forget living in a castle.

Yet apparently that was exactly what she'd done.

Her door opened, and a man held out his hand to help her out of the car and into a waiting wheelchair. "Welcome home, madam," the man said and attempted a smile. Two other men, clearly security, waited on either side of the front door.

The ground floor of the mansion, at least what she could see en route to the elevator, was amazing. Pure elegance even a visiting royal would appreciate. They wheeled through the marble and glass foyer, then slipped by the huge living room to the right and a dining room that could easily seat four dozen people on the left. Beyond was the kitchen. She smiled and waved at the staff who had come out to welcome her home. They looked at each other in surprise. One hesitantly waved back. Before she could ponder that odd reaction, she, Wade and the attendant who pushed her wheelchair were inside of a small elevator, and for the first time, she caught a glimpse of herself in the mirrored walls.

There were few words that could describe the reflected image. *Horrible* was one. *Appalling* was another. It was so not her. Her hair hung in long, limp tendrils. Her face was still pretty banged up, although the bruises were fading to a relatively nondescript yellow. Her left eye was bloodshot, and she could see a slight, almost healed cut on her bottom lip. The swelling was going down. She patted her face. Overall, she looked like she'd been in one whale of a fight and had not been on the winning side.

There was a soft *ding*, and the doors opened onto a wide corridor, the floor inlaid with beautiful white and gold-embossed marble tiles. The attendant wheeled the chair to the right and followed the hallway almost to the end, finally turning into a large bedroom. It was done in pastels, primarily in varying shades of green. Very nice. Very soothing. Very bland.

"Does this suite suit your needs?" Wade asked from the open doorway.

"Yes. It's great," she replied. "It's…big." The spacious room had a separate sitting area on the far end, with comfy-looking chairs surrounding a fireplace. French doors opened onto a huge terrace. There was even a bar with a small fridge. A luxurious bed with silk wrappings completed the effect.

"Do…you…stay in here as well?"

He watched her almost as though he was measuring the question, and she thought she saw a spark of devious temptation flash in his eyes. "No. My suite is next door."

A feeling of relief rolled through her. At the same time, it struck her as odd that a newly wedded couple would have separate bedrooms. More than likely he was letting her have her own room, thus giving her space and time to readjust rather than push her to move directly into the master suite. And she was grateful. She wasn't ready to share a bed with a strange man despite her attraction. And regardless of any marriage certificate that might say otherwise, he *was* a stranger.

Standing up from the wheelchair, she walked around the room, looking at the paintings and art objects decorating the space. Most of the paintings were by renowned artists, some of which she recognized. There were pictures of flower gardens and old ivy-covered stone walls and gates.

"Either you or your designer has very good taste."

"You know art?"

She shrugged. "I recognize Monet and Barber. And I guess I know what I like."

"Do you?"

She pivoted around to face him. Her heart skipped

a beat at the look of sensuous suggestion on his face, in his voice. She had the distinct impression he wasn't talking about fine art. Was he flirting with her? Establishing his claim? Or had her imagination overtaken her common sense? Still…he was her husband. Maybe he was reminding her of that fact.

Not sure how to respond, she turned to look at the painting hanging over the mantel. A little girl with long reddish-blond curls stood in the corner of her room, presumably being punished for something she'd done. Her dog, a little brown terrier, stood guard against anyone who would come near his child. A name flashed through her mind. *Murphy.* She turned to Wade. "Is… Murphy here?"

A sharp frown met her question. "Who?"

"Murphy."

The gracious warmth of his welcome instantly turned to icy cold foreboding. "There is no one named Murphy in this house."

His clipped reply indicated she'd struck a nerve. But why? Who was Murphy? Why did she remember that name when there was no face to go with it?

"I have work I need to take care of. Henry, our chef, put a menu next to the phone. I have taken the liberty of arranging your first meal based on the foods you generally like. If it isn't acceptable to you, feel free to order something else. Call the number on the bottom of the menu once you've made your selection."

"That was very thoughtful. Thank you."

"Your mother's phone number is on your bedside

table in case you don't remember it." With a sharp nod, he left the room, closing the door behind him.

What was that all about? She had no idea why simply asking about a name would cause such a change in behavior. His sudden hostility caused regret to surge through her. Apparently there was someone named Murphy who stood between them. It wasn't a good feeling. How could she remember that name and not remember her own husband? A numbing chill slid over her. Was another man the reason Wade had acted so distant?

A soft knock on her door brought her out of her worried contemplation.

"Yes? Come in."

The door opened to a stout young woman in a nondescript black dress and shoes.

"Excuse me? Mrs. Masters? I'm not sure if you will remember me. I am Rowena. Roe. Mr. Masters asked me to assist you with anything you need."

"Oh. That's very thoughtful. Thank you, but I'm fine."

The maid hesitated before saying, "I hope you feel better very soon." Then she backed out of the door.

"Roe?"

"Yes, ma'am?"

"I think… Could I change my mind? Would you mind helping me draw a bath?"

"Yes, of course, ma'am. I'd be happy to." She hurried past Victoria and disappeared into the bathroom.

Victoria ventured into the huge closet while Roe

started the bath. It was lined with clothing for every occasion. Many garments still had the price tag attached;
others were still in the designer's bag. Shoes filled one
wall, and in the built-in bureau, there was lingerie in
every style and color.

She was a clothes hog. It looked like she'd bought
more clothing than she would need in a year. Maybe
two.

"Your bath is ready, Mrs. Masters."

"Thank you." She smiled at Roe. "You're very kind."

That earned her a surprised, wide-eyed stare from
the housekeeper. "Thank you, ma'am."

Grabbing a robe, she ventured toward the elegant
powder room, then on to the beautiful marbled bathroom. The oversize jetted tub couldn't have been more
appealing if it had been edged in twenty-four-carat gold.
Across the room, a glass shower large enough to hold
five looked equally tempting. But right now, she wanted
to soak away the hospital smell. The dull ache in her
head persisted, but hopefully the warm water would
take care of it. Soon she was lying back, eyes closed,
as the hot jets of water massaged away the soreness
from her bruised body. She grabbed the liquid soap
she'd selected from a wide array of bath salts, soaps
and shampoos in a cabinet. Soon she was inhaling the
wonderful exotic scent and enjoying the sense of clean-
liness it offered.

When her fingers began to get pruny, she knew it was
time to get out. After toweling dry, she slipped on the
fluffy white robe. She found both a comb and a brush,

plus a new toothbrush and some toothpaste in one of the drawers. Standing in front of the large mirror, she combed the tangles from her long dark hair.

As she looked at her reflection, a feeling of unease passed through her. Something was off. It was probably just the bruises and cut lip. She turned her face to the side. Maybe some swelling remained. "Stop it!" she muttered to her reflection. She had enough to worry about without adding to it.

"Are you all right, Mrs. Masters?" Roe called from the bedroom.

Excellent question. Placing the comb back in the drawer, Victoria headed to the bedroom. With the succulent smell of the food being wheeled into the room, she let the internal quandary go for now.

As good as the food looked and tasted, she did little more than sample a couple of the dishes. Her appetite had disappeared along with any positive hopes that coming here—coming *home*—would rekindle her memory. So far, all it had served to do was add more unknowns to the growing list. She felt tired and melancholy. Her husband's earlier reaction to her inquiry about the name stirred apprehension. Everything she thought she would find here was still missing. In fact, she had an overwhelming sensation that she didn't belong here. In this house. She couldn't explain it, but the feeling was strong.

After the food cart had been removed, she found a clean nightgown, pulled back the covers and sat down on the bed. She really should call her mother. Even though she didn't remember her.

Finding the number written on a sticky note, she placed the call.

"Hello?" a woman answered.

"Hi, Mom. Mother." *What did she call her?* "It's me, Victoria." There was an obvious pause on the other end.

"Oh, my dear. You don't sound at all like yourself. Are you still in the hospital?"

"No. No, I'm at home."

Another pause. "Are you telling me that man dumped you off at his house and left? That might be a cause of action for abandonment or mental distress. You really should speak with Burt as soon as possible."

What was she talking about? "Uh…Wade has been with me the entire time. He's still here."

"Oh. Well, we will just have to think of something else. Sooner or later Wade Masters will screw up and he'll pay for it dearly, if you get my drift. If you can find a private moment, it wouldn't hurt to call Burt anyway. Maybe he can think of another angle."

An angle? For what? "Who's Burt?"

"Why, your attorney. How could you not remember *him*? Do you really have amnesia? Wade said you couldn't remember anything. You're making me nervous, Victoria. You need to get over this memory thing before you say or do something that Wade will use to boot you out the door. Call Burt's office. He needs the information on the driver who hit you, his insurance and such. Look, sweetheart, I really must go. We'll talk again soon."

"Uh…okay." And before Victoria could make sense of any part of the conversation, the line went dead. How odd. Not once had her mother inquired as to how she was feeling. And all that about calling an attorney. What was that? She had no info about the accident and had assumed Wade would take care of it.

She hung up and eased into bed. It felt good to lie down. The silk sheets were amazing, the mattress and pillows so soft, especially compared to the bed at the hospital. Her vision again fell on the painting above the mantel. What was it about the painting that called to her? Surely Wade would know. But was it somehow related to what had caused his hostile reaction earlier?

She still had the dull throbbing in her head, though it wasn't bad enough to get up and take one of the pills Dr. Meadows had prescribed. She didn't know if it was caused by the accident, being in this strange unwelcoming monstrosity of a house, or Wade's show of anger and the anxiety she'd felt at his reaction. But neither the bath nor putting some food in her stomach had eased the pain totally. Maybe when she woke up everything would be back to normal.

Whatever *normal* was.

Three

Wadding another piece of printer paper into a tight ball, Wade tossed it against the far wall with the idea of bouncing it into the trash can below. There were significantly more small white balls on the floor than in the basket. He didn't care.

She could bloody well remember the name of one of her lovers but not her husband? That was a hell of a thing to admit. His irrational irritation continued to mount as he sat at his desk, trying to drum up sufficient enthusiasm to concentrate on the work in front of him.

Of course, she wasn't really his wife in the biblical sense. And considering their history, he really shouldn't be surprised or affected either way. But she had drawn him in with the sweet, innocent act, then waylaid him when he wasn't expecting it. One minute she seemed so innocuous…so…*not* Victoria. Those lilac-blue eyes—which had never seemed so blue—radiated such warmth, need and an almost childlike innocence. She'd silently implored him to help her. Then in the blink of an eye she was dredging up memories of some man. It was Victoria at her best. He snatched another sheet of paper from the printer tray. If ex-lovers were what it took to help her memory return, they definitely had a problem. He didn't know all their names, and he didn't care. But they were not going to visit her here. Just the thought of it had him again gritting his teeth. Another ball sailed through the air. Another miss.

He ran a hand over his mouth, sat back in the chair and took a deep breath. This entire situation had begun as one of those *Why didn't I think of this before?* ridiculously brilliant ideas. Or so it had seemed at the time. Victoria's father had given her a taste of high society before he lost everything by making foolish moves in commodities trading. Even when she had been poor as a church mouse, she had continued to maintain the facade of wealth and privilege, which was exactly what Wade had needed: a beautiful woman who knew how to dress and function skillfully at social gatherings, and who epitomized a billionaire's wife. In that regard, Victoria was exceptional. She could even do *happy* if he pressed her on it. What she couldn't do was *discretion*. He'd soon discovered Victoria didn't know the meaning of the word.

Wade had long ago stopped longing for a wife, someone he could love, trust and raise a family with. Twice he'd fallen for a woman who had seemed so sincere, so earnest, only to learn it was all a ploy to gain money. After the last time, he'd called an end to it all. Bitter and discouraged, he refused to again put his heart on the chopping block.

Now, because of the accident, it was as though Victoria had a complete change of personality. And apparently that change had a far-reaching effect, because he'd sure been snagged and reeled in. It seemed that, in the blink of an eye, she'd gone from a wife-in-name-only with a cardboard persona to a three-dimensional woman he found extremely hard to resist. He knew an illogical desire to be near her, to be with her and protect her. His mind raced to curb visions of him holding her close through the night. It was crazy. A mere three weeks ago, the last time he'd been in Dallas, he couldn't stand the sight of her.

How could he never have noticed how slender she was, how tiny her waist? How perfectly her breasts suited the other contours of her body? When she'd walked around her suite, her hips swayed enticingly, something he should have noted long ago. Had her lips always been so full and luscious? He'd never been physically attracted to her in the past. Yet the thought of her lying in his bed gave him insane ideas of forgetting all about the parameters of their previous relationship and making love to her with such wild abandon it would cause her to forget the names of her lovers and cry out his name instead. Such notions had never entered his mind in the almost five years he'd known her. Why now? Hell, maybe he was the one who needed to see a doctor. He crinkled another sheet of paper in his hand before it joined the others on the floor.

He had to get a grip. Such thoughts were completely ridiculous—outrageous and totally inappropriate under the circumstances. She'd just come from the hospital. Still, when their eyes had met in the private hospital room, for the first time he'd seen honest emotion there, something he hadn't thought the woman capable of. And against all reason, his body had responded. Then today, in the limo, he'd encountered her sense of humor. Who knew hidden away under all the glamour and glibness Victoria Wellington Masters actually had a sense of humor?

He couldn't explain why he suddenly wanted to be close to her. He couldn't rationalize it, but he had to accept the reality of it. That was half the battle. A man couldn't fight something until he acknowledged its existence. So, okay. Fine. He now found something about her appealing. Quite a few things, in fact. Heaven help him. But he would not give in to this insanity or be suckered into her little games. Despite the way his body reacted every time they came close enough for him to inhale her scent, in spite of his eyes being drawn to her full, enticing lips and the delicate features of her face, he would bide his time, keep those lunatic feelings to himself until she was fully healed, at which time she would be escorted out the door. And all this would be nothing but a bizarre memory.

He wouldn't ask her to leave, certainly not until she'd fully recovered, even at the cost of his sanity. But he damn sure wouldn't lay himself open to becoming involved with Victoria. His face was already hitting the front page of the tabloids, the kind that exploited the secrets of the rich and famous. Headlines like Does Her Husband Know About the Other Men? or Who's Been Sleeping in Victoria's Bed—Lately? were a dime a dozen. Victoria had sworn she was dating only one man. She had been making an earnest attempt to keep their affair under wraps. Perhaps the tabloids were pulling from old photos. Though it was hard, maybe he should give her the benefit of the doubt.

She kept an apartment in North Dallas. He didn't know the location but imagined it would be easy enough to find. If returning to familiar surroundings would help her memory, they would definitely make a trip there. Add it to the top of the list. She'd never stayed in this house more than it was necessary to keep up appearances. She'd never shared his bed. There had never been anything about her that had tempted him to want to get closer. Until the damn accident. The sooner she regained her memory and signed those divorce papers, the better.

Pushing the work aside, Wade grabbed the phone, dialing his attorney's private line before settling back in the black leather chair.

"Wade." The voice on the other end held surprise. "What's going on?"

"I think we may have a problem."

An hour later, Wade hung up. He'd been right. There was no way a document signed by a person with confirmed amnesia would hold up in court. He had no choice but to wait it out and hope her mind righted itself quickly. Hell, that was a scary thought. At least she wouldn't be going out in public anytime soon, so his main worry was leashed for the time being.

Wade booted the computer and waited for his mail server to appear. He might as well try and get something done. When her memory returned, he intended to be waiting, documents in hand.

Victoria tossed and turned and plumped her pillow, and still sleep refused to return. The clock on the nightstand said 2:40 a.m., some twenty minutes later than the last time she'd looked. She sat up, knowing she wouldn't be going back to sleep anytime soon. More than likely it was due to the strange surroundings—even though they shouldn't be strange to her.

Throwing back the covers, she swung her feet over the edge of the mattress and stood up. Opening the French doors leading onto the terrace, she stepped out into the warm night air. She immediately heard the sound of water spilling over rocks. Soft, diffused light filtered through the trees and highlighted a water feature. Leaning over the railing, she spotted the huge waterfall and a rock-lined stream that wound through trees and out of sight. What castle would be complete without a waterfall? And what had Wade done with the moat?

The soft floral scent of roses mixed with lavender reached her on the light evening breeze. She would have to go down and explore in the daylight. But she didn't see any chairs or other places to sit in the manicured garden below. Wade needed to get a bench so they or their visitors could sit outside and enjoy the beauty.

A fast knock on the door to her suite pulled her attention away from the calming scene. She headed back inside and was halfway across the bedroom when the door opened. Wade stood in the doorway, his dark hair tousled as though he'd been running his hand through it. He wore sweats and a baggy top that revealed signs of moisture, as if he'd been working out. His mouth was drawn into a tight line, underscoring the fatigue that showed in his eyes. Behind him, two of his security staff stood poised and ready for anything that might go wrong.

Upon seeing her, Wade visibly relaxed.

"Were you just outside?"

"Yes. I woke up and couldn't go back to sleep, so I stepped out onto the terrace." She frowned. "Was I not supposed to?"

"No, it's fine," Wade assured her, rubbing the back of his neck. "All the outside doors and windows have silent alarms that are activated overnight. In future, please call security and let them know your intent so they don't see it as a break-in. Just hit pound six on the landline phone."

"Oh…okay." She glanced past Wade's broad shoulders at the two men. "I'm sorry. I didn't know or, if I knew, I didn't remember."

They smiled and nodded. "That's not a problem, ma'am."

When her gaze returned to Wade, that look of surprise was back on his face.

"You seem to be feeling better," Wade pointed out as the two security men left.

So do you, she thought. At least as far as his attitude went. "I am. I just wish my mind would catch up with the rest of me."

"I'm confident it will in time."

"I was looking at your garden." She pointed toward the French doors. "Below the balcony? It's beautiful. The sound of the water falling over the rocks is so relaxing. But I didn't see a bench or any place to sit."

Wade readjusted his stance. "A bench? No one ever goes back to that area."

"Maybe it's because there's no place for them to sit."

He looked dumbfounded. "I suppose that's possible."

She shrugged. "Why have the flowers and the waterfall if no one ever sees them?"

He stared at her like he'd never seen her before. As though she was an apparition and he didn't quite know what to do about it.

"Yes. I…see your point."

But he was frowning.

The character lines framing his mouth were tantalizing. She'd bet he had an awesome smile—so far, she'd caught only slight glimpses of it. She would love to run her hands over those indentations and kiss his full lips. He would be a great kisser. She didn't know if it was a memory or female intuition, but she knew it all the way to her core. A vortex of heat suddenly surrounded her, making her breath shallow and her heart rate speed up considerably.

"Well, um, I'm sorry I triggered the alarm. I'll do my best to remember to call the next time." She needed him to leave so she could turn on a fan.

"Not a problem." For countless seconds he stood in the same place, just watching her, as if his feet wouldn't obey his command to leave. Then his brain must have repaired the connection, because he blinked, shook his head slightly and turned toward the door. "Have a good evening."

"Wow," Victoria muttered to the empty room when he was gone. She had no idea where she'd found him, but at the moment, despite his earlier anger, she was very glad she had. He still didn't act like a husband in love with his wife. Maybe it was a case of him not knowing what he should or shouldn't do regarding her injuries. Surely, as they became reacquainted, that would change.

The morning light sifted into the room through the sheers drawn across the floor-to-ceiling window. Slowly Victoria stretched, yawned and sat up. Tired of robes and hospital gowns, she wanted her jeans and a comfortable shirt. In the closet she found some designer stretch jeans. No T-shirts, but an ample selection of blouses to choose from. Unfortunately, all the shoes and boots appeared to have four- or five-inch heels. *Ugh.* She wasn't up to that and, really, she shouldn't have to wear such things in her own house. She'd just go barefoot. The decision felt right. After securing her long hair in a ponytail, she ventured into the hall and paused, trying to decide which way to go.

The garden. She'd see if she could find it. She elected to take the stairs instead of the elevator. The grand circular stairway ended in the foyer. Maintaining her sense of direction, she turned and walked toward the back of the house. Surely there was a back door.

And there was. It opened at her touch, and she stepped outside into the morning light. Just ahead of her was a huge pool with a hot tub. It was surrounded by natural stone, banana trees and other exotic plants, which gave it a tropical feel. To the left was the huge waterfall, with more tropical ferns and plants growing at its base. Following her instincts, she rounded a corner of the mansion, and there it was: a floral garden set into an alcove.

It was even better from here than from the terrace. Peeking into the water that formed a stream at the base of the falls, she spotted beautiful gold, red and white fish. She didn't know how she knew, but these were koi. She knelt down on the thick grass and watched them with delight. Between the concentrated scents of various flowers and the roar of the waterfall, she felt more relaxed than she had since leaving the hospital. Stretching out on the luscious lawn under the rays of the morning sun, she closed her eyes.

* * *

No one had seen her leave. She'd all but disappeared. What was Victoria doing, and where was she doing it? While the housekeeping staff searched inside the house, Wade followed a hunch that led him outside. As he rounded the back corner, he immediately spotted her. Lying on her back in the grass with one arm thrown over her eyes, she appeared completely relaxed. It was a sight he'd never imagined seeing. Victoria was not one to embrace nature in any size, shape or form. Apparently that had changed. At least temporarily. He noted she wore no shoes. Perhaps a call to Dr. Meadows was warranted?

Wade approached slowly, not wanting to startle her, but needing to know she was all right.

"Victoria?"

"Hi," she responded but didn't move. "This is so great."

"We do have chairs."

"Not out here. Only around the pool. You don't have a bench, remember?"

She had him there. "No. No bench."

Using her arms, she pushed herself into a sitting position. "I think over there, under that tree, would be the perfect place to put one." Intending to scramble to her feet, she winced and grabbed her left side, the site of the bruised ribs. Pushing on, she got to her feet and walked over to the place she'd suggested. "About here. You can see the waterfall and most of the flower beds from this location. It's shielded by water ferns and banana trees. It's quiet, private and beautiful. What do you think?"

Wade wasn't sure what to think. Her behavior was anything but normal for Victoria. "Yes. I agree. It looks like a perfect place."

He watched as she once again lowered herself to the ground. "Come and join me." She patted the grass next to her.

Hesitantly, he ambled over and looked around for an alternative place to sit.

"Sitting on the grass won't hurt you."

"It won't help either," he muttered, then lowered himself to the lawn. He couldn't remember the last time he'd sat on the ground. She was right: it wasn't bad. He was surrounded by the smell of rich earth and flowering plants. Images sprang to his mind of the ranch where he and his brothers had grown up. The rolling hills, the unbelievable palette of color in the fall, trail riding for days, campfires at night. It was long ago, but those memories he would keep forever. Their mother had insisted her brood be raised in the country, believing a child needed to feel a bond to the land. His father had reluctantly agreed, so their sons had grown up on a ranch, learning about cattle and beef prices and what it took to operate a spread of enormous size.

He had always envisioned raising a family on the Masters ranch. He pictured his wife loving it there as much as he did and their kids spending their days on horseback exploring the countryside. In his early years, he'd hoped to find someone who shared his heart as well as his dreams. Finally, he'd given up and made himself settle on a wife that shared nothing except what was required in the contract. A facade for all to see.

"Victoria, do you remember any part of your past? Childhood? Adolescence?"

"Intermittently. I have mental glimpses of people and things. Like I recognized the Dallas skyline. I don't know how I knew it was Dallas. I just knew." She was quiet for a few moments. "I think I used to work with my hands." She held them up in front of her face. "They feel…empty." She sighed.

This was the first he'd heard of such a thing.

"And I'm pretty sure I used to like being outside."

"*That* I can assure you was not the case. At all."

"No?" She frowned and seemed to let the thought roll around in her mind. "I've been getting these feelings that just seem…right." She glanced at Wade. "I can't explain it better. I wish I could. But being here, outside, feels right."

Wade didn't have an answer to that, so he didn't try. "Sit up and let me see your face," he said.

The bruising was almost gone and the cut on her lower lip had pretty much healed. "Better," he stated and was gratified to see her smile. "How do you feel, generally?"

"Good," she said and looked up into his eyes.

Less than a foot separated them and the temptation to lean toward her and put his lips against hers was overwhelming. *What was wrong with him?* This was Victoria. How out of place was any temptation to touch her? She raised one hand and placed it against his cheek and he shuddered at the sensation.

"You have such a handsome face," she whispered. Her gaze lowered to his mouth. Wade could feel himself harden at both her touch and the implication of her words.

Pure lust shot through his body as his mind fought to hold on. As hard as it was to believe, he wanted her.

"Your lips are very…"

Wade's tentative hold on his self-control grew thinner. His hands cupped her face, and he eased her toward him. For an infinitesimal moment his face remained a breath away, his lips open, ready to taste her. He wanted to kiss her. Hell, he wanted to do more than that. His subconscious mind screamed *no!* Just behind her moist lips, perfect white teeth guarded the nectar he knew he would find there. He could feel her soft breath on his face, saw her eyes close as if in preparation for his kiss. Heaven help him. Slowly he placed his lips against hers, and the grip on his desire slipped away.

He pulled back and for a few seconds fought to hold on to the control he desperately needed. The raw hunger for this woman rose in his gut. This was insanity. He could not—*would* not—be attracted to Victoria. He damn sure wouldn't have an affair with her. She would use it against him eventually, somehow. Yet all he wanted to do was make love to her right there. Near the flowers she apparently loved. Right in front of God and everybody.

Anger at his own weakness overcame the temptation.

He rolled to his feet. She was watching him, a look of confusion in her eyes. He took a deep breath and tried for normal.

"Have you contacted your mother?" he asked after clearing his throat.

She frowned. "Yeah," she whispered, then took a deep breath. "It was awkward. I didn't know how to address her."

Victoria claiming she didn't remember that vile woman could be a good thing. Still, he knew when the memories came back, more than likely her mother would be among them.

"Wade, why did you—"

He cut her off. "It was a mistake. I shouldn't have kissed you."

"I was going to ask why you stopped." Victoria lay back on the soft grass. "Please don't go."

Pheromones shot through his body, and it took most of his strength to refrain from going back to her. His body was hard, tense. He needed a release. Dammit, he needed Victoria.

"I have a meeting." And if he didn't get away from her soon, he would never make it to that meeting.

"That's too bad. I think you need to relax occasionally. And I think you would enjoy daydreaming in this beautiful garden."

"Daydreaming doesn't allow much time for business."

She looked at him, a smile warming her face. It was the first time he'd seen her without anxiety and pain marring her delicate features. Or the mask of disgruntlement she normally wore. It was the first time a freshly scrubbed and exceedingly beautiful Victoria had actually smiled at him rather than smirked.

"That's too bad. Really."

There was absolutely no way Victoria would normally sit outside on the grass under the shade of a tree. Let alone smile about it. He would definitely take it up with Dr. Meadows when they went in for her appointment.

"I'd better get back inside. The meeting is in about half an hour."

She wiggled to a more comfortable spot on the ground. "Here? At the house?"

"Yeah."

"What's it about?"

He couldn't help looking at her to see if she was joking. Victoria had never shown any interest in any aspect of the business, not that he would have let her be privy to much of the information. As long as the contractual installments that kept her here were paid on time, she couldn't care less how the money was earned. It was odd that she'd asked. But what about this entire situation *wasn't* odd?

"We've just received all the clearances for the resort we're preparing to build in the Caribbean. I'm meeting with the architect and the designer to finalize the plans for the cottages."

"That sounds like fun."

"Fun?" He scratched the side of his face. "I never really looked at it as fun."

"Might as well like it if it's something you have to do." She shrugged. "Thank you for coming to look for me."

In the five years he'd known her, he had never heard the words *thank you* leave her mouth. He was pretty sure he'd never heard Victoria say those words to anyone. Her mind-set was one of privilege. She expected people to wait on her, and in her mind that didn't require any thanks. He could get used to this new Victoria.

He brushed off his slacks and bid her good day, heading back to the door. He couldn't help but wonder what else would be revealed on her journey to wellness and how much longer this new Victoria would be around.

Four

Dinner that evening was held in the dining room. The forty-eight-seat table kind of put it in perspective: her husband had yet to discover the world of casual. But the food, when it was served, was delicious. She closed her eyes, savoring the taste of the fresh Maine lobster. "My gosh. This is so good," she said, not waiting until she'd chewed and swallowed.

"I'm glad you find it to your liking." There was an unmistakable glint in his eyes.

She nodded her head. "How'd your meeting go?"

"Okay. It was just a formality to finalize plans for the resort. John provided an artistic take on the landscaping, and Mac reiterated the completion dates."

"Landscaping?" A picture flashed in her mind. A

woman sitting in a windowsill, behind her a glorious sunset as she smelled a rose, a soft smile on her lips. Victoria's head throbbed with the memory.

"Yeah." Wade took another bite of his lobster. "The final idea seems off to me, but I couldn't say what is missing or what, if anything, needs to change."

She nodded, taking a sip from her water glass, hoping the throbbing in her head would go away on its own.

"Would you have any interest in seeing the sketches? Maybe you can spot something we missed. You seemed to enjoy yourself at the waterfall today and had good ideas about putting in some seating."

Her gaze shot to his face. "Me? You want me to look at them? Seriously?"

"Yeah." He shrugged. "Why not? Unless you don't want—"

"Yes. I'd really like that." He was reaching out to her for the first time. He was offering her a glimpse of his world. It was a small step toward rebuilding their relationship, maybe even a few steps in the direction of trust.

They ate in silence for a while. Victoria looked around the massive dining room, at the wainscoting, the three crystal chandeliers above the table and the forty-six empty chairs. It was so formal.

"Do you...*we* always eat in here?"

"In the past, you've preferred it." His answer was dry, like he didn't necessarily share her taste for it.

"Isn't there a kitchen?"

He raised one eyebrow, indicating her question was

absurd. "I believe we have one, yes. That would be where the dinner was prepared."

"I mean, does it have a table?" she pressed. "Something smaller than this? Or a bar? You know, with stools? A place where just a couple of people can sit and eat. A place not so formal."

Wade looked perplexed. It was as though the idea had never occurred to him or he'd never expected her to make such a request. And now that she'd said it, she wasn't at all sure why she wanted somewhere unpretentious. After being married to Wade for eight months, she should be used to this type of formality.

"I believe we do."

She refocused on her plate. "Have you ever had all these chairs filled? Like, at the same time?"

"On occasion."

"That's a lot of pizza."

He stopped with his fork halfway to his mouth. His lips pursed at the unexpected humor. Clearly, he remembered their previous joking about his family business being a pizza joint.

"It is. And we serve only the best. But no jalapeños," he said in a serious tone.

"Agreed. Or anchovies."

"Or anchovies." He finished taking his bite of food.

"How long have you lived here?"

He patted the linen napkin against his mouth. "It's actually the family home. My grandfather started the business and did well enough that he had the core building erected before he died. My father later added the west and east wings. It works well for meetings that last several days and provides enough space for guests to stay without going to a hotel. The business associates visiting from other countries especially seem to prefer to stay here."

"When they're not here…it's a big house for just two people. Do you ever get lonely? Do I?"

He shrugged. "You've always seemed to manage. I've been staying here off and on most of my adult life. I guess I've never really thought about it. I have other houses, an apartment in New York, a villa outside of Rome, a flat in London. I stay in whatever area my business requires."

"So…you're here now because of me?"

"Primarily."

Why did that realization make her a bit sad? What important things had he had to cancel because of her?

She glanced at him as he returned his focus to his plate. He was so incredibly male. A tuft of hair hung over his forehead. Combined with the tanned face and dark features and the way he sometimes looked at her, he clearly gave off the impression there was a bad boy inside just waiting for a chance to come out. It was a total contrast to the proper, ever so polite Mr. Masters persona he strove to make people see. It was a look that said he could eat her up and still stick around for dessert. She'd had the same thoughts this morning when he'd kissed her in the garden. That kiss may have been soft and tentative, but it would have quickly grown to hunger he couldn't hide or easily control. She had to wonder if he ever let go of the rigid restraints he maintained and let raw passion determine his actions. Let the beast inside free. She took another sip of her water, determined to keep her imagination at bay.

"What about your family? Any brothers or sisters? Parents?"

"Both parents deceased. I have three brothers. All younger. Cole is also involved with the business, just a different facet of the corporation. Chance is recently retired from the military and runs the ranch in Calico Springs. Seth lives in Los Angeles. We all try to get together a couple of times a year or whenever possible. Haven't seen Seth in a couple of years. We stay in touch by phone or Skype."

"You all grew up here? In this house?"

He shook his head. "No. Actually, we lived on the ranch." He hesitated as if wondering whether or not to say any more.

"Please go on."

"My…mother came from a ranching family. She learned early on to respect the land, and she was determined her sons would grow up in the same environment. Apparently Dad finally agreed, so, just before Chance was born, he built a house on some land his family owned. We attended the local schools and grew up checking out the wide-open spaces on the back of a horse. Seth is a half brother and was born and raised in LA."

Wade rested his elbows on the table and linked his

fingers. His gaze was directed at the far wall, but Victoria sensed in his mind he was a long way from here.

"Mom and Dad both believed a person should work for what they had and were determined for all of us kids to know the value of a dollar. Since we were living in Mom's playground, those lessons were learned by mending fences, feeding the livestock, taking on the general responsibilities of ranch life. Later, after college, Dad introduced each of us one by one to the world of business. One day led to another and here we are."

"You've never gone back? To the ranch?"

"I did for a while. But it's been close to a year."

"I think you should go," Victoria encouraged. "I think you should take a week—or more—and revisit your memories. See if you can still saddle a horse."

Wade laughed and the glitter of amusement shone in his eyes. "Maybe I will."

"What…" She cleared her throat. "What did I do while you were away or working?"

Wade laid his fork down on the plate and seemed to give her question some thought. "I don't think you did…anything."

"That's crazy." She frowned, placing her fork across the gold-rimmed plate. "I had to do something. I mean, no one can just sit around and breathe day after day."

Wade shrugged. "You went shopping. Went to the hairdresser. Visited your friends. I really don't know."

Now it was Victoria's turn to look shocked. "I didn't work? Didn't help a charity? Arrange garage sales? Dig holes? *Nothing?*"

"Victoria, we didn't really see a lot of each other. On average, I spend more than half the year traveling. When I'm not out of the country, I'm in meetings or working in my office in the city, where I also keep an apartment. Occasionally we do attend a social gathering together, but even then, you have your acquaintances, and I have mine."

She was speechless. She couldn't imagine living the life he described. It sounded horrible. For a married couple, it just didn't make any sense. Somehow she knew within herself she was not the type to hide away day after day in this big house. And Wade had to take some downtime and enjoy life occasionally. No one could live as he'd described for years on end without paying for it physically, if not emotionally. Everybody needed time to relax. To laugh. To dream.

As she watched him eat his dinner, she realized she wasn't seeing a man who was happy and content with the world in which he lived. She was seeing a man who marched to the drum his current life demanded. He was staying well away from any friends or relationships that would take his time away from his business, including his own wife. The question was *why*. He was polite to a fault, handsome, rich…and very much alone. Why had he married her? It was like the dog that finally caught the car it had chased for years. Now that he had it, he wasn't quite sure what to do with it.

It was just sad. Period. All of it. How he rarely returned to his childhood home and had little to no personal contact with his brothers except, she assumed, in emergencies. Flying around from one country to another and never realizing a true home... Maybe she could plan something to get his family together.

She took one last bite of her dinner, laying the fork on her empty plate. "This was excellent. I didn't realize I was so hungry."

An older man came into the room and politely inquired if either one would care for dessert. Victoria placed her hand over her stomach and declined. "I'm stuffed."

"None for me either, Jacob. Dinner was good, thank you."

The man nodded, took the plates and left the room.

"Do you feel up to looking at those design renderings?"

"Sure." Her headache still had a dull throb, but it was slightly better than earlier today. She refused to let it keep her from sharing this time with Wade.

Together they walked down a long corridor. His hand was resting on the back of her waist. It felt odd, but not unpleasant, to be guided through the colossal home by this man. He stopped in front of double doors and opened one side for her. Like everything else in this house, his office was huge. Wade went directly to a side table and picked up a plastic tube containing the drawings. He removed them from their carrier and spread the sheets out on his desk. She walked over and stared at the first composite drawing. Wade was right. Something about the balance was off. As to the color, there wasn't any.

"Are the cabanas going to be white?"

"Yeah," Wade said, stepping closer until she could feel the heat from his body against her back. "More of a cream. The idea is to use them as a kind of palette for all the colors found on the island. The tropical plants contribute color at ground level, and I believe someone said there are over three hundred bird species, including parrots and macaws."

She realized she was once again shrouded in a warm vapor of sensation that was getting hotter by the second. She shook off the beginnings of arousal his closeness was causing, fighting to ignore the sexual response her body was determined to set in motion. She looked at the next few drawings, forcing her mind to stay on them. The cottages were primarily adobe-style with small variations around the entrances obviously intended to make each unique. But even with different doorways and variations in landscaping, they looked the same.

"What do you think?" His tall, muscled body pressed against her as he gazed at the sketches over her shoulder.

"These are very nice."

"Nice," he repeated. "Victoria, tell me what you think." His warm breath caressed her ear, his voice— that deep, rich baritone—causing shivers to run across her skin. Anxiously she reminded herself to breathe.

Shaking her head, she pivoted around from the drawings and found herself wedged between Wade and the table. The top of her head almost touched his chin, requiring her to look up into his face. His gaze found hers and for countless seconds neither moved.

She gave a slight shrug. "Who am I to be giving advice on multimillion-dollar vacation complexes?" It was almost a whisper, but it was the best she could do. "I don't even remember my own name." His mouth was so close, so tempting. He had a sexy five-o'clock shadow that only served to reinforce her earlier reaction to his masculinity. The feeling of warmth spread through her body like a wildfire fanned by the wind, causing her breasts to swell and her breath to become shallow. She couldn't help but stare at his lips: so masculine, so tempting.

He slowly lowered his head, bringing his lips only inches from hers. A little warning bell sounded in her head, reminding her that she was about to start something she wasn't sure if she was ready for. And if she crossed that line, there was no going back. While he was her husband, she still didn't know him. She didn't know what their relationship had been like before the accident. She clenched her hands into fists, determined not to place them against his chest, stand on her tiptoes and press her lips to his. With more strength than she thought she had, she turned back to the sketches.

She glanced down at the desk and took a deep breath in an attempt to fight off the growing desire to be in his arms.

She cleared her throat. "If you want the cottages to meld with the island, I would think you would paint some of them a rich sandy brown reflecting the color of the beach. Others could be a pale peach or light orange—pick up the colors in a tropical sunset and maybe a dark turquoise representing the water. The flowering plants will still be striking against a colored wall as long as the blooms aren't the same color as the walls. Also, each cabana has a private courtyard." She pointed to the area. "To me that screams *hammock with a coconut cocktail*. If you can find any hammocks made locally, consider adding one or two to each cottage. Comparatively, I don't think it's a big expense and the visitors might really enjoy it. I know I would. I think."

She felt his hand slip across her back and cup the side of her waist as he leaned closer to the drawings.

"And here—" she pulled out another large sheet and placed it next to the one on top, determined to keep herself from melting at his touch, his masculine scent "—they have palm trees centered in front of each cottage. They look…planned. Plant them in small groups at either end of the house and change the positioning with each cottage. Make them look random, like they're part of the natural element there. I would think the very last thing you would want in a posh resort in the Caribbean is cookie-cutter anything."

She could feel his gaze on her face. When she looked around, she was caught by the intensity of those brown eyes. A heated blush encompassed her face. "I'm… sorry. I shouldn't have said anything. Don't pay any attention to me."

"That's all I seem to want to do," Wade said softly, his voice gravelly as he tipped his head and lowered his lips to hers. "Pay very close attention to you," he said against her mouth.

She couldn't have moved if she'd wanted to, and she didn't. Her total focus was on Wade and the look on his face that held her captive. His full lips drew her in, and she clutched his shirt with both hands, wanting more, holding on for dear life. A small whimper left her throat when he pressed his lips against hers. Then he drew back before kissing her again, harder, determined. His mouth opened over hers, and his tongue pushed inside, exploring, filling her. His hands rose to cup her face. She could feel his breathing becoming fast, could sense his intense emotion taking her own body to a new level.

Too soon he lifted his head, breaking the contact as he looked deeply into her eyes. She sensed he was going to kiss her again, but instead a frown covered his handsome features, and he drew back as if weighing the wisdom of his actions. As he continued to hold her face in his hands, his eyes lingered on her lips.

Something in his eyes made her sense that he regretted getting this close to her. Although she didn't have a clue why, that suspicion was confirmed when he took a step back and turned away. His mouth set in a straight line. She swallowed hard, feeling awkward and exposed.

She wasn't sure what to say, so she said nothing. With one last glance at her husband, she hurried to the door.

"Victoria…"

Gathering herself, she stopped just inside of the door. "I think cream cottages will be very nice, just the way your designer has it," she said without turning around. "They are lovely just as they are."

With that, she made for the elevator.

"Wait. Victoria," Wade called.

She kept walking. Still feeling the moist throbbing low in her belly, she fought the temptation to go back and do something really stupid.

She had to be realistic. The sky was the limit on what had happened between them before the accident. For all she knew, they were in the final stages of a heated divorce. Come to think of it, that would certainly explain why he'd made no move to touch her before, why he was so distant and, at times, gave her the distinct impression he didn't even like her. She wished he would just come out with it and tell her what had come between them.

Not that it would necessarily make her any readier to share his bed if theirs was a true and happy marriage. Although, after what she'd experienced five minutes ago and this morning, he wouldn't have to try very hard to convince her. At least she would know where she stood in his life. If he wanted a separation, a divorce, she was doing well enough physically that she could move on. She didn't have to stay here. Surely she had some type of skills that would earn a position somewhere?

She stepped into the elevator and sensed the same awkwardness as she'd felt the day she arrived. The renewed frustration of having no memories plus her body's strong reaction to Wade before he turned away increased the volume on her headache. By the time she reached her room, it was full-blown. She hurried to find the bottle of pills.

It was time she and Wade talked. Really talked. If

she was a burden, if there was no love between them, she needed to leave. Before she fell in love with her husband.

Wade stared at the door Victoria had closed behind her. What in the hell was he thinking? Never had he entertained the idea of kissing Victoria. Before the accident, if it had so much as crossed his mind, the very idea would have been ridiculous. She was undeniably attractive, yes. But he'd never been even remotely attracted to her. She met the requirements as far as being the perfect wife for a billionaire: beautiful, poised, charming when the situation demanded. Victoria had no compunction about her role as his pretend wife. Nowhere was it written or assumed they had to genuinely like one another. They rarely saw each other. Any attraction would have been one-sided on her part and, as far as he knew, that was not the case either. Yet since she'd awoken from the accident, he had been inexplicably drawn to her. He would watch her lips as she talked almost to the point of not listening to what she was saying. Her eyes were the shade of the irises his mother used to grow in her garden. Blue with a hint of lavender, amethyst. They were fascinating. How had he never noticed her eyes before?

As he turned, his gaze fell to the drawings on his desk. Her suggestions were remarkable, and he would definitely pass on her comments to the designer. But it only added to the growing list of suspicions he had about her behavior. Something about her was off. There had to be a catch, something about her he wasn't seeing. This whole new persona had to be fabricated. *Had* to be. There was no other viable explanation for it. In the years they had known each other, but especially in the months since she'd agreed to the sham marriage, this was the first time she'd ever shown any interest in what he did. The fact that she'd made suggestions—good suggestions at that—blew his mind.

If she really was faking the amnesia—whatever her game plan—she was doing a number on his psyche. The closer he got to her, the closer he wanted to be. By the time she'd finally begun talking about the drawings, he was as hard as a steel girder. *Damn.* In those moments when he'd looked into those eyes, he was past caring *why* he was suddenly attracted to her. Hell, what did it matter? He wanted to taste her. He wanted to be inside her. Hell, he wanted a lot more than that. Desperately, he wanted Victoria to stay the way she was right now, memory or no memory.

Never in his previous relationships had he experienced the desire he now felt for Victoria. The cloud of suspicion for most women that had come after Cynthia, his fiancée of two years ago, was slowly evaporating, something he hadn't thought possible. His throat tightened as long-repressed memories of their final moments tore at his mind. Cynthia had even gone as far as to claim she was pregnant. All in a staged effort to ensure that a marriage between them would come to pass. Then weeks before the wedding her father had stepped forward, admitting his daughter's scheme. The devastation he'd felt at Cynthia's betrayal still brought back the anger.

Victoria had always viewed others as inherently inferior. Her quest for permanent acceptance within the circles of the rich had hardened her. She'd become ruthless in her determination to regain her family's previous status and had turned into the cold, cynical person she was today. Or at least the person she was before the accident.

Some of the questions she asked intrigued him. She had appeared completely surprised when he'd told her that she didn't hold down a job. Working at anything was unthinkable to the Victoria of the past. He knew she was a clotheshorse, always dressing to perfection. Sometimes she even set a fashion trend with one of her styling ideas. But the way she looked at those sketches…her approach was almost professional.

Her actions were becoming more unusual by the day. Could a knock on the head cause a person's basic character to completely change? It was almost as though she had a dual personality thing going on. He definitely needed to speak with Dr. Meadows, but since it wasn't an emergency, it could probably wait until her scheduled appointment. Until then, all he could do was to wait and watch. If she was acting, sooner or later she would slip up. It was inevitable. Like a kid, he had his fingers crossed in hopes that the wicked witch wouldn't return. Yet, at the same time, he needed some answers.

He'd racked his brain to try to figure it out. If this

was a hoax, what was the payoff? It would have to be about money. With Victoria, it was always about money. But he hadn't come up with one solid idea of what she might be up to. Yet.

Five

Prior to going to bed, Victoria stood in her bedroom, staring at the picture that hung over the mantel. She still didn't see anything in the painting that reminded her of anyone. It was 80 percent background, and the only subjects were the child and her dog. The artist, Charles Burton Barber, had signed the painting in the lower right-hand corner. So why did it bring the name Murphy to mind? There was no reasonable explanation. She took in a breath and blew it out in yet another sigh of frustration. Memories were churning in the back of her mind; she could almost feel them spinning around and around, searching for a way to come out. How could she open the door and let them?

A soft knock on the door broke her concentration.

"Come in," she said, wondering who could be knocking on her door so late.

The door opened, and Wade stood on the threshold.

"I just wanted to make sure you were okay. You left rather suddenly." He tipped his head in question, and his gaze held hers.

"I'm fine." She shrugged. "Thank you for letting me look at the drawings. The resort will be incredible."

He paused for a long moment as though considering saying something else. Then he nodded. "I hope so. And your insights will be passed on. I think you were right on." He bumped the door frame with his left fist. "All right, then." He gave an affirmative nod. "Have a good night."

"You as well."

Victoria gave up searching her mind for answers and got ready for bed. Lying on the soft mattress in the darkened room, she couldn't stop herself from reliving the earlier moments in his office. The warmth of his body against her back. The way his lips moved over his strong white teeth when he spoke. She hoped he would kiss her again. Long and slow and deep. Damn this memory thing. Only a few more days and she would see Dr. Meadows again. And she wouldn't be short on questions.

Everything was moving in slow motion. Multiple shades of red splattered on the glass in front of her. She couldn't see out. She couldn't tell who was behind the pane. She tried to sweep the colors away, but that served only to swirl and mix them into an insipid, lifeless gray. Shards of glass flew about her head, lingered in the air above her before turning and heading straight down, each one piercing her skin with the precision cut of a razor.

She heard a scream. Over and over, someone was screaming. Was she the only one who heard it? She had to go for help. She had to find someone to help, but she couldn't move. Then she was again looking in the glass that had transformed into a mirror. She watched the blood run down her face as the sound of a siren filled the space around her. Everything was distorted. The world was spinning upside down. The face in the mirror was talking, but she couldn't understand the words. Over and over she heard a man's voice telling her he would free her from this place. He kept telling her to hang on. But she was so tired. The pain in her head was unbearable. Better to give in to the darkness. But she had to breathe. She had to fight for the next breath. If she gathered enough air in her lungs, she could scream and someone would hear her. But the blackness was stronger than she was. Like a wave coming to shore, it rolled over her, soothing her, giving her peace. She had to hang on. *No! Please no!*

She felt the warmth of strong arms around her. The darkness began to recede. She buried her face in the muscled shoulder of the man who held her as she cried, the sobs uncontrollable, as was the trembling that tore through her body. She held on to him, needing his strength, afraid he would leave her alone again.

"Victoria." The reality of Wade's deep voice broke into the nightmare. "It's all right. Come on, hon, wake up. You're having a bad dream. You're safe."

His soothing words and the warmth of his body as he held her began to diminish the fright of the nightmare. Blinking open her eyes, she saw the increasingly familiar surroundings of her suite. She was in her bed, with Wade holding her safe and protected. She should feel embarrassed that she'd apparently awakened him from his own sleep, but the warmth and safety she felt as he held her close overruled any idea of pushing him away or putting up a front of bogus bravery. The dream had held her in its horrifying grip until Wade had forced it away and brought her back to reality. She took a deep, shaky breath to calm the last of the tremors.

"It was so awful," she whispered, her cheek against his naked chest. "I couldn't move. I couldn't breathe."

His arms tightened around her, then one hand began to soothingly rub circles over her back. "I heard you cry out."

Her mind wouldn't let her recall everything, but she remembered the vivid colors of red everywhere. She had been in so much pain. Was it the accident? Was that what had happened to her?

She sat up then, moving away from his chest as reality fully set in. Her gaze roamed the handsome features of his face. With tenderness, he wiped away her tears.

"Wade, I—"

Her remaining words were reduced to an unfinished thought when Wade leaned down and his lips found hers. Briefly. A feather-soft meeting. He drew back, watching her, and she thought she saw a battle going on in his eyes. She reached up to touch his face, tracing the character lines that only added to his potent allure. With a deep moan, he kissed her again, this time more forcefully, moistening her lips with his tongue, demanding entrance to the deeper secrets of her mouth, and Victoria didn't think of resisting. His hand grasped the back of her head, holding her to him as his tongue pushed inside, hungry, seeking.

It was an explosion of sensation. He tasted of coffee, a hint of vanilla and a whole lot of hot-blooded male. His mouth covered hers enticingly, drawing back before returning with even more vigor. His lips were simultaneously soft and firm, enveloping her own, yet she could sense the passion he held tightly in check. His natural masculine scent surrounded her, stimulating her own need with every breath, making her hunger for more. In that moment, she wanted only to lose herself in his arms.

She felt weightless, then the softness of a cloud touched her back. Her body grew hot, the heat centering at the apex of her legs. Every thought in her head floated somewhere in an abyss.

Absently, she realized her head was against a pillow, his hands cupping her face while his lips and tongue continued to stir the passion pooling hot and deep in her belly.

His body was over her, his erection hard and almost painful as it pressed against her belly. She squirmed in a frantic effort to move so he would be at her opening, where she desperately needed him to be. For a minute in time, he helped her, repositioning himself against her core, the barrier of her panties the only thing keeping them apart.

Suddenly, with a groan, he pulled back and sat up, leaving her confused and wanting. Breathing hard, he watched her in the soft, indirect glow from the lights in the garden below. The muscles on his jaw moved in rapid succession, and regret covered his features.

He stood from the bed and ran a hand through his hair.

"Damn. I'm sorry, Victoria." His voice was husky.

Before she could answer, Wade turned and walked out the door.

Victoria fell back against the pillows. What just happened? She inhaled a deep breath and blew it out in an effort to slow her racing heart. At least she knew without any doubt that passion was still very much alive in their marriage. Maybe she could get him to talk about what happened that had apparently put a wall between them. Or, if he was merely concerned about hurting her, she would make sure the doctor assured him she was fine. Because she was.

She pulled the covers up to her neck. The room suddenly seemed cold. In fact, she'd felt the chill as soon as he'd withdrawn his arms.

Why had he apologized? Was it because he'd almost made love to her? Or because he'd stopped? One thing stood out in her mind: he wanted her. For now, that was enough. For maybe the first time since the accident, she had hope. Memory or no memory, maybe they could work it out.

What in the hell had he been thinking? *Goddammit.* He didn't give a hot damn about her lovers or any other aspect of her personal business, as long as it didn't affect his own. So what in the hell was he thinking when he'd kissed her? Even worse, he'd kissed a woman who didn't even remember who he was. She was barely out of the hospital after sustaining a major concussion. She needed to be able to trust him, at least until her memories came back. And he'd pounced on her like some love-starved jackass. He'd taken advantage of her having a nightmare. How pathetic was that?

Entering his own suite, Wade closed the door behind him, ambled across the room and fell onto the bed. This was not good. He didn't know what had changed between them, had no idea why suddenly Victoria had become so appealing. But she had. He'd felt the change growing since she'd batted those baby blues at him in the hospital. He'd shaken it off as just human compassion for another who was hurt, frightened, and needed his help.

That rationale had been blown to hell when she'd invited him to sit on the ground under a tree. *Him.* The Wizard of Wall Street. Wade Masters, revered financial genius, sitting on the ground under a damn tree. And—worse still—he'd liked it. It took him back to his childhood, to the memories of growing up on the ranch with his brothers. The tricks they would play on each other. The camaraderie.

He had not wanted to stop kissing Victoria, even though he knew it was the wrong thing to be doing. He was playing into her hands like a blind fool, and until he could figure out what she was after or prove she was lying about the amnesia, he had better pull himself together. Every second spent in her company was a step deeper into her web of deceit. The only hope he had was to get her out of this house and permanently eliminate the temptation to take their relationship to the next level.

His attorney had cautioned Wade about doing anything she could claim would be placing her in danger, meaning she had to be healthy and fully capable of taking care of herself before he asked her to leave. If Dr. Meadows gave her the all clear in spite of the memory loss, some time spent on the family ranch might be just the ticket. Despite her urging him to revisit the ranch and her little sit-in-the-grass party, he knew damned well Victoria didn't like nature or anything remotely outdoorsy, regardless of how much she was pretending otherwise. She had a distaste for animals, and zero appreciation for anything country. He still hadn't figured out why she was pretending to enjoy things totally out of character. She had to be scheming. The big question remained: *What was she after?*

Maybe the answer would be revealed after she'd washed and groomed a dozen horses and mucked out a few stalls. Taking her to the ranch seemed like the perfect plan. Push enough country living in her direction, while he relaxed in his favorite place in the world. Something would give, and it wouldn't be on his end.

Whatever had happened to Victoria in that wreck, he would not let it affect him. He couldn't afford to. He'd leave all of her peculiarities to a psychiatrist to try to figure out. From now on, he would stick to his office and keep the damn door closed. Or, better yet, leave. It was a little over a week until her doctor's appointment, and he had more than enough staff to see to her needs. There was some business he honestly needed to address in New York. Without further consideration, he picked up the internal phone and dialed the house manager.

"Curtis? Yeah, I need to fly to New York for a couple of days as soon as it can be arranged."

"Yes, sir. The plane is fueled and ready. I'll contact the pilot. I can have a car sent around to the front… Give me two hours on everything?"

"Perfect. Thanks. Oh, Curtis? Something else."

"Yes, sir?"

"Victoria… Take her shopping. She's been complaining about not having comfortable shoes. Take her to a few of the better clothing boutiques. Tell her I said to get whatever she wants."

"Yes, sir."

He'd known if he ever let emotions enter his life, his neat and orderly existence would go to hell in a handbasket. But…was it emotion that caused him to want to be close to Victoria? Taste her lips? Feel the warmth of her breath on his face? Hear her whispered sighs as he held her close? Emotion meant he had to feel something for her.

Feel something for *Victoria? Oh, hell no!* It was animal instinct. Purely sexual. Even that was a stretch of the imagination. This was Victoria he was thinking about.

This was the third time in as many days she'd suckered him into whatever game she was playing. Regardless of whether it was on purpose or not, despite how much he'd enjoyed kissing her, it damn sure would not happen again.

The next morning at breakfast Victoria was advised by a man who introduced himself as Curtis Shepherd, the house manager, that Wade had been forced to return to New York for some urgent business. Wade had asked him to pass on his apologies and assure her he would be back in time for the appointment with her doctor. A nagging suspicion had her wondering if Wade really did have urgent business. Or had he left to avoid her? The idea made her uneasy and a little sad. Was it possible Wade had not seen their passion the previous night as a positive thing? A step toward rebuilding their marriage? She hadn't had the opportunity to talk with him about their marriage. The subject of why it might be in trouble wasn't a conversation she'd wanted to bring up. But it was making her crazy. She had to know. When he got back, they were going to discuss it.

Curtis also told her Wade wanted her to go shopping for shoes and anything else she needed. Curtis was to accompany her, driving to the stores she used to frequent. It was nice of Wade, but the only thing she needed was a good pair of sneakers, and that hardly seemed to be worth the man's time.

Finishing her breakfast, she decided she would go on a mission of discovery. Between the house and the estate grounds, there was so much to see. It seemed like the perfect opportunity to refamiliarize herself with this gigantic house.

Her first stop was the kitchen. The chef and his two assistants were busy turning out what would no doubt be another spectacular dinner. Surprised by her presence, they were immediately uneasy. She had to assume it was because she'd come into their area of the house. Finally, after she gave them plenty of compliments and ready smiles, they began to loosen up and seemed only too happy to explain what they were preparing, their words conveying such pride in their work.

An idea began to form. Maybe one of the chefs would know of a smaller, more intimate area they could eat, instead of that huge, formal dining room. She turned to the one who was most proficient in English, even though his thick French accent still made him difficult to understand. He gleefully took her to a diminutive alcove between the hall to Wade's office and the elevator. The area was just big enough to fit a table and a couple of chairs. Maybe a plant for ambience? A floor-to-ceiling bay window filled the far wall, framing a water fountain just outside. The only piece of furniture there was a sofa. It was perfect. As soon as she could have a small table and two chairs delivered, she wanted all future meals to be served here.

Eventually, she found herself back at the elevator. Returning to her room, she placed a call to Curtis and gave him her request. A small table and two chairs would be delivered tomorrow along with one ficus tree. Curtis suggested the area where she wanted to place the new furniture might need repainting, and they'd want to remove the sofa. Victoria gave the go-ahead, excited to see how it would all come together. She especially wondered how Wade would like it.

Curtis also politely reminded her of the shopping spree. She didn't know if it would be a *spree*, but she would go and get a new pair of shoes. They made arrangements to leave at two that afternoon.

When the time came, Curtis and two security guards met her at the car. Two hours later, Curtis pulled the car back into the circle drive. Victoria got out with two bags, both containing everyday casual shoes.

Her spirits lifted, she dumped the two boxes inside her closet, slipped on a bikini and headed for the pool.

The flight back to Dallas seemed endless. Never before had Wade felt like pacing during a flight. He knew Victoria was the cause. He was actually looking forward to seeing her again. That was a first. He was probably setting a new world's record for foolishness.

"We are in the flight pattern for landing, Mr. Masters," the pilot spoke from the cockpit. "ETA about five minutes."

Good. For the first time in…maybe forever, Wade looked forward to returning home. After a perfect landing and a quick switch to the waiting car, he was on the last leg of his journey. It was well past midnight. He was tired and irritated. His stay had lasted longer than expected. The meetings hadn't gone well, primarily because he'd not been prepared. He'd left half the documents on his desk back in Dallas and couldn't keep from constantly wondering what Victoria was doing. For the first time that he could remember, he vehemently did not want to conduct business. And then it had been a long flight home, made even longer by his internal agitation.

The next day was Victoria's appointment with Dr. Meadows. Wade had refrained from calling him about Victoria's bizarre behavior, and he wasn't sure why. Maybe it was that some of her new quirks he rather liked. In all honesty, he didn't want her to revert back to the woman she'd once been. It wasn't fair to her, granted. She deserved to have her memories and her life back. But still…

"We're here, Mr. Masters," the driver said before stepping out and opening the door for Wade. "I'll have your things cleaned and the luggage stored. Have a good evening, sir."

Wade made the appropriate reply and headed to a small side entrance of the house that not everyone knew about. To a stranger, it would not appear as an entry at all, since the door was hidden behind an evergreen. He'd taken this path so many times he could do it blindfolded.

From the driveway, there was a series of stepping stones through the landscaping to the carefully hidden door.

The first stepping stone felt strange under his foot. The second one even more so. It was as though the flagstone had been removed, which was ridiculous. The third stride almost took him down. He recognized his problem: he was standing in pure mud. *Where in the hell were the paving stones?* On the fourth step, the mud encased his foot up to the ankle and had him fighting for his balance. Struggling, he finally managed to take another step forward, but his shoe remained behind. He groped the air for something to hold on to seconds before he fell to his knees. His briefcase was claimed by the darkness as he determinedly fought his way to the side door, finally reaching the concrete entrance by crawling on all fours like a dog.

Standing on the small cement step, he looked back in the direction he'd just come. From this angle, Wade could see that someone had indeed removed the stepping stones and apparently decided quicksand was more to their liking. But who? Who would do this? Victoria's face flashed in his mind like an image on a big screen. *Nahhh.* Why would she do something like this? Landscape design wasn't her thing.

Wade entered the security code, pulled open the door and stepped inside. Reaching down, he removed his one remaining shoe and both muddy socks. His slacks were in no better shape, so he ditched those, too. With grim determination to keep a tight rein on his temper, he set out for the elevator. He'd not gone far when he tripped over a large obstacle directly in his path. Wade felt himself go down in what seemed like slow motion, his feet tangled in God knew what. The sound of wood and metal hitting the floor echoed down the empty hall. *What the hell?* What was a chair doing in the hallway?

Clambering to his feet, he didn't notice the table until his head hit the bottom of it, setting off another series of bangs and crashes as it fell onto its side. Levering himself carefully to his feet, he righted the table and once again turned toward the elevator. He never saw the potted tree that stood more than double his height until he and it were waltzing in the dark. He finally fell against a wall that prevented him from losing his balance yet again.

Suddenly the lights came on, and he was able to view the obstacle course he'd just come through. Two wrought-iron chairs with wooden seats, a matching table and a damn tree. He noticed traces of white covered his hands and the sleeves of his suit jacket. The pungent smell of fresh paint reached his nose. The chef stood in the kitchen opening, his eyes as big as saucers. No doubt the noise had echoed all the way through the kitchen and into the employees' section of the house.

"Get this tree out of the middle of the damn hallway," Wade barked at the man, who scurried to do his bidding. With a scowl, Wade limped to the elevator.

When the elevator doors opened to the second floor, he cut a beeline directly for Victoria's door. And this time he didn't pause to knock.

And there she was, sitting up in bed reading a book, a

look of pure innocence on her beautiful face. She looked up, obviously surprised by his late-night visit. Then her eyes quickly went wide as she took in his appearance.

"Wade?" Frowning, she threw off the covers and hurried toward him. "What happened? Where are your pants? You're...covered in mud. How did you tear your shirt?" Reaching up, she pulled a small, six-inch-long twig from his collar. "What's on your suit? It looks like white paint all over the back of your jacket... Oh dear."

"*Oh dear?* Did we do a little shopping while I was gone?" His jaw worked overtime. "A little rearranging?"

"Yes." She had the decency to grimace. "I bought two pairs of shoes and...the little dining room was supposed to be a surprise."

"Let me assure you, in that you succeeded."

"We didn't have a small table for meals, so I bought one, along with two chairs to go with it. Remember? We talked about it that night during dinner. And you were right. I found a perfect area for just the two of us to eat, but no furniture." She bit her bottom lip. "Curtis thought it might need repainting. So I told them to just put the furniture in the hallway. And the ficus."

"The what?"

"The...the tree. It's a ficus tree. The painters needed room...to work." She narrowed her eyes and frowned. "Actually, I don't really understand how you could have missed seeing the tree. It's about twelve feet tall and almost as wide."

"I know. Believe me. But I can't see trees—or furniture—in the dark."

"In the dark? Was something wrong with the lights?"

"No."

"I don't understand."

He took a deep breath, determined to keep it civil. "It was dark because I didn't turn on any lights. I didn't think I needed to. It should have been a simple walk to the elevator, one that I've made countless times."

"Surely you're not blaming *me* because you didn't bother to turn on any lights?" She looked incredulous. "And the hallway would have been clear if you'd come back when you were supposed to. You weren't scheduled to be back until tomorrow."

She was right, but he refused to allow her to turn the tables on him. "Did you remove the paver stones between the driveway and the house?" He heard the growl in his words.

She nodded. "I had help, but yes, I did. I needed them moved in order to plant a garden."

"A garden."

"For fresh vegetables. I didn't want to dig up the lawn," she explained as though those were the only two options she had. "All I saw was bark chips and some stepping stones that led nowhere, which seemed rather pointless to me."

"They led to a door. It's intentionally hidden."

"Then why do you have stepping stones leading to it? Isn't that a dead giveaway?"

Wade ran a hand over his lower face, remembering all too clearly why Victoria had her own place in the city. "Tomorrow perhaps you can help me understand the need for a vegetable garden? It isn't like we have no food in the house," he barked. He could hear the frustration in his own voice and tried to rein it in.

He took a deep breath and turned to leave, not willing to stand there one moment longer covered in mud, half naked at one o'clock in the morning and debating the need for a vegetable garden. The top of his head was still tender from the encounter with the table. All he wanted at the moment was a hot shower. There was no doubt she had set this up. She was pushing him to lose his temper. She had to be. He just didn't know why. A move to the ranch was looking better and better. She'd be well-advised to watch out. Paybacks were hell.

Six

The door closed behind Wade. Victoria looked at the twig she still held in her hand. She was honestly sorry he'd experienced a problem coming into the house. A problem of her making. But he really wasn't supposed to have gotten home until tomorrow. Or technically today. She'd intended to have everything set up and ready to surprise him at dinner tonight. Well, she'd surprised him, all right. Just not in the way she'd intended.

She returned to her bed and set the book aside. Turning off the bedside light, she lay back on her pillow and stared into the darkness. One thought ran in circles through her mind: after this long, she was still the stranger here. Regardless of how hard she tried, she still managed to cause havoc, either by setting off alarms or making well-intended changes to this house. Everything was so formal it was difficult to breathe. How she'd ever spent eight months in this house doing nothing, especially with Wade gone most of the time, was something she couldn't imagine. She could relate to the old adage about the bird in a gilded cage. And nothing she did seemed to make any difference for the better. And how could it ever? She lived in a perfect house with a perfect man. She consumed perfect food and slept in a perfectly soft bed. She didn't like perfect. She certainly wasn't perfect and was pretty sure the real world wasn't either.

She'd been counting the hours until Wade returned, imagining his smile when she showed him the changes she'd made. Instead, everything had blown up in her face. By the look of him, Wade was really mad. She supposed he had a right to be. But he must know she hadn't intended to sabotage him. Actually, she'd intended just the opposite.

She slid off the bed and padded to her door, then continued to Wade's suite. A moment of hesitation had her almost turning and running back to her room, but she held firm. Reaching out, she knocked on his door. No answer. She knocked again, this time a little harder.

Suddenly the door was wrenched open, and Wade stood in the doorway, one towel slung low over his hips while he blotted the moisture from his head with another, grimacing when it touched the top of his head.

Before she could open her mouth, he stepped back into the room and disappeared around the corner, leaving her to choose to come in or to turn around and leave. Taking a deep breath, she stepped forward into the lion's den.

"I just wanted to apologize," she called out, hoping he could hear her. "It never entered my mind that…well, that you would come home early. Or at night. Or that you wouldn't turn on the lights. Or that there was an entrance there, and you would use it." She huffed out a sigh. "You could have called and told me, and none of this would have happened."

Wade stepped back around the corner, still wearing the towel. His thick dark hair was damp from his shower, softly curling about his head as though it refused to be tamed. His broad shoulders filled her vision. The sleek muscles of his chest and arms moved under tanned skin with oiled precision as he brought his hands up to rest on his waist. "This is how you apologize?" His eyebrows rose, a spark of challenge in his eyes. "Saying the debacle downstairs was my fault?"

"No. I'm to blame for what happened. Ultimately. I'm just pointing out you could have avoided it."

"You'll have to pardon my disagreement, but calling home to announce my arrival so a tree can be moved out of the way from the center of the hallway is not normally on my list of things to do."

"Which is why you should have turned on the lights."

Wade opened his mouth as if about to argue, but no words came out. Instead, he closed his eyes, shook his head and uttered a sigh.

"I'm sorry you got paint on your suit coat. I hope the dry cleaners can get it out. Where are the pants?"

Wade's mouth was set in a straight line. His eyes narrowed to golden-brown beams as he caught her gaze. He stepped toward her and the urge to retreat was strong. Wade was a powerful man, in more ways than one. She was surrounded by an incredible scent of hot clean male, and there was little between them but her flimsy nightgown and a towel barely hanging on his hips.

Rather than frightening her away, his gaze held her in place.

Stopping a mere foot away, he said, "I don't think this is about lights or the tree or whether or not I should have called."

Victoria frowned. "I don't understand."

"Don't you?" He reached out one arm, his hand cupping her face, his thumb rubbing gently over her cheek. With little effort, he drew her to him.

His thumb traced the line of her lips and his gaze lowered to watch the movement. Her heart was doing cartwheels, and her breath stalled in her throat.

Wade closed what little distance remained between them and lowered his lips to within a breath of hers. "I think maybe you were trying to get my attention. Rest assured, it worked."

"No, that's not at all—"

"The next time, just tell me what you need, and I'll make sure you get it. It's more direct and involves a lot less drama. In fact, it's not too late." He nodded his head toward the large bed.

His mouth covered hers, devouring her lips, seeking the deep recesses of her mouth. His hand cupped the back of her head, ensuring she didn't move away. She had no desire to do anything other than respond to the heat he was causing throughout her body and the moisture pooling between her legs. His mouth was hot, his tongue exploring the cavern of her mouth. His arms encircled her, and he pulled her tight against him, causing his granite erection to press against her stomach. With a little moan, her hands found his bare shoulders, and she answered his need. She was quite sure she'd never been kissed in such a manner or by a man like Wade Masters. He was amazing. He knew exactly what she wanted and proceeded to give her more. How could she have forgotten moments like this?

"You make it very hard to remember you're injured," Wade whispered against her lips, his voice rough. Then his mouth covered hers in one last, lingering kiss before he raised his head and took a step back. "Go. Go back to your room while you can. I'm trying damn hard not to pick you up and…" He took a shaky breath. "Go, Victoria. Now."

Victoria backed to the outer door, turned and all but ran down the hall to her suite. God, how she'd wanted to stay in his arms. She trudged to her bed and climbed in, pulling the covers around her. Visibly shaken, she knew she was walking a razor-thin line between making love to her husband and denying them both until she could remember him and what transpired between them before the accident. The way she felt right now, she wished she'd just said *no* to his demand she leave and stayed exactly where she was—where she wanted to be—in his arms. In his bed.

As far as she could tell so far, he was the man she'd always dreamed of. Not his wealth. Not his power. Just Wade. The man. Purely the man. What had she done to make him want to keep his distance? And how would they overcome it?

Dr. Meadows closed the door behind him and extended his hand first to Victoria, then to Wade. He set a small laptop on the counter and powered it up. "So, how have you been, Mrs. Masters?"

"Good." Victoria smiled at the good doctor. "My ribs are still a little tender, but not bad."

"Headaches?"

"Yes. Some. But they are manageable for the most part. And they don't happen very often."

"And the memory? Any improvement?"

"Not really. Maybe a quick flash of an image or a name here and there."

"Are you able to retain those images?"

She nodded. "Yes. But I don't understand any of them. I don't recognize them."

"She is experiencing some changes in her personality." Wade spoke up.

"Like what?"

"Basic likes and dislikes. Opinions. Her interests seem to have shifted." Wade stood in the corner, his hands thrust deep in the pockets of his slacks. "She likes going barefoot. She enjoys sitting on the ground. Outside. Under a tree. Before the accident, she wouldn't be caught dead doing that."

"It's pleasant. You should do more of it," Victoria countered.

"She doesn't want to go shopping. I had to leave instructions for my houseman to take her shopping and I was told, even then, she didn't want to go."

Wade turned a frustrated glance to Dr. Meadows. "And she planted a garden. She had one of the employees remove paving stones and landscaping and plugged the space full of tomato plants. Do you understand what I'm saying, Doctor?" Wade rubbed the back of his head. "We don't need tomatoes!"

Dr. Meadows stifled a grin and looked down, rubbing his forehead.

"Mr. Masters, while I can appreciate what you're saying, sometimes amnesia can cause a person to temporarily change their core values, their likes and dislikes. It doesn't happen very often. But I must say, in all honesty, if my wife staunchly refused to go shopping, I would consider myself a very lucky man."

He trained his sights on Victoria. "Do you have any memories associated with what you like or don't like?"

Victoria looked at her husband, then shook her head. "No. As I explained to Wade, some things just feel right. I can't offer a reason other than that."

"While it's not a common occurrence, it is possible with a traumatic head injury such as you sustained. We can't rule anything out." He turned to face Wade.

"I would suggest just being supportive of your wife's new interests, as long as she sticks to growing tomatoes and doesn't start robbing banks."

She couldn't stop the small snort of laughter. She dared a look at her husband and received a stern glare. Apparently Wade didn't share in the humor.

"I would like to see you again in about three weeks, just as a precautionary follow-up. We'll do another MRI and see how things are looking on the inside, but I don't anticipate anything negative. You seem healthy otherwise and I see no reason that you can't return to your full activities. It might even help with memory recall."

"Great." She hopped down from the table. "Thanks, Dr. Meadows. I'll be here on the eighteenth for the MRI." She turned at the door and watched as Wade shook the good doctor's hand before accompanying him down the long hall and out the front door. When they stepped out of the building, she felt the summer sun on her shoulders. She glanced at her husband. He appeared deep in thought.

"Wade?" she said. "I know my cell was destroyed in the accident, but why do I have no friends? I mean, not one person has called or come to see me since I've been home. I talk to Mother on occasion, but she doesn't seem to have the time or the desire to discuss it. She says I'm being silly to worry about it. Keeps telling me to stick to the business at hand…whatever that means. Getting my memory back, I suppose."

"Of course." He didn't sound convinced. "I'm afraid I can't answer your question, Victoria. I don't think you had very many that you considered close friends. Perhaps they will come around in time. Unfortunately, I don't have names or numbers to give you."

That seemed strange. Surely her husband would know the name of her best friend? Theirs was truly an odd lifestyle. Or so it seemed. But she had no concrete foundation to base her suspicions on. Perhaps it was just the way life was.

When they arrived back at the mansion, Victoria headed upstairs, and Wade made his way to his home office. He closed the door and sank down in the leather chair behind the desk. Reaching for the phone, he dialed the number to the ranch. It was answered on the second ring.

"Triple M Ranch," a woman cheerfully answered.

"This is Wade. Is Chance around?"

"No, sir. He has gone to a cattle auction in Oklahoma. He won't be back for a couple weeks. But Holly is here. Or at least at her vet clinic."

"I'm bringing my wife out for a short stay. Could you have someone freshen the Pine House cabin?"

"It will be wonderful to see you again, sir. We will have the house and vehicles ready to go. Do you have a general idea of when you'll be arriving?"

"Toward the end of next week."

"Excellent. I'll let Holly know you're coming, and we'll see you then."

He sighed and ended the call. Every day they were together he felt drawn to Victoria more and more. But

Wade had to give her some leeway while she healed, not press her on the return of her memories. But the time was drawing near. He knew sooner or later she would revert to the Victoria he knew, and giving any thought to consummating their marriage would be setting himself up for a hellacious time when she regained her memory. Sharing a bed at the ranch wasn't going to help to put distance between them. In fact, it was going to be damn hard to keep from making love to her. Victoria saw him as her husband. Not a cardboard replica of a man whom she married on paper only. She didn't know that part, and he was hesitant to tell her. Would it shock her memory into returning? Or would it just shock her, period? Maybe the news would have no effect. Yeah. Probably not. He knew this Victoria well enough to know that if it didn't bring back her memory, it would most certainly disturb her.

He exhaled a deep breath. He was ready to put his plan into action. He'd use the horses, the campfires, the hiking and anything else he could find to send Victoria running back to Dallas after admitting her memories had returned. It had been hard enough staying away from her the times they had been together. He would shut his mouth, keep his distance and stay alert to any further changes in her demeanor. If Victoria had honestly changed and discovered a love of the outdoors, she would get her fill at the ranch. If she was pulling some type of con, the ranch would have her confessing in no time. High-society types like her did not normally fit in with cowboys, cattle drives and longhorn steers.

A glance at his watch said it was past two o'clock. Wade took the elevator to the second floor and knocked on Victoria's door. After several minutes he knocked again. This time the door was thrown open. "Hi."

"Uh…hi." Wade swallowed hard. Victoria was standing before him clad in only the briefest neon-yellow bikini. Her dark brown hair was pulled back into a knot. "I was about to head down to the pool and get some sun."

"I wanted to see if you'd care to have lunch."

"Sure. Let me throw on a T-shirt and pants—or is a dress needed? Are we going out?"

"Casual will be fine. I'll wait. Go ahead." Wade strolled into the room while Victoria raced for the closet. Uncharacteristically, her suite was as neat as a pin.

He expected the wait time to be at least ten minutes, but before he could sit down, Victoria was back, dressed and ready to go. She'd even put on a pair of shoes.

They made their way downstairs. When Victoria turned to go into the dining room, Wade took her arm and directed her toward the kitchen.

"Where are we going? I thought you said we were going to eat here."

"We are."

Victoria couldn't hold back the surprise when they turned left and stopped in the entrance to the alcove. The table and chairs she'd bought had been placed in the center of the cozy space, and the table was set with dinnerware for two. The tree was to one side of the window. The water feature outside had been turned on, its droplets glowing like crystals in the afternoon sun.

The full smile on her face was breathtaking.

Wade cleared his throat and seated her at the little table. Victoria simply could not keep the smile off her face. "Thank you, Wade. I mean that."

He shrugged. "You did all the work. You selected the table and chairs."

"Actually, Curtis did. We picked them out together from a catalog, and he placed the order. Even the tree."

"Bless him for that," Wade said, straight-faced but slightly sarcastic. "Well, whoever was responsible for getting them here did good. And this is hands down better than eating in the formal dining room." He sat back in his chair. "And I'm going to enjoy the view as well as the meal."

He looked directly at Victoria, and she lowered her head, refusing to meet his glance. Not the normal response for Victoria, who sought out any and all attention whenever she could find it.

"But the next time you redecorate, remember to put up some signs warning of construction."

She nodded her agreement. "And turn on some lights for through traffic."

Jacob chose that moment to approach the table. "Are we ready to dine, sir?"

Wade nodded. "I believe we are."

The old butler disappeared for a few minutes and returned holding two large flat boxes. He set both in the center of the table. "Here we have a meat lover's with pepperoni and sausage." He moved it to the side and opened the other box. "Here we have a sampling of meats and vegetables. I believe this is a Supreme. No jalapeños or anchovies."

Victoria burst into laughter.

"Thanks, Jacob," Wade said, grinning.

"You are most welcome." He turned to Victoria. "I'll be right back with your salads. Uh…dig in."

Surreal. She'd even had a positive effect on the staff.

She grabbed one slice of each pizza and placed them on her plate. Picking up the pepperoni and sausage slice, she took a sizable bite and rolled her eyes, muttering, "Oh man! That is *so* good."

Wade helped himself as he continued to watch his wife enjoy her meal. In the past, she'd rarely shown such enthusiasm, even for a filet mignon prepared by a world-renowned chef accompanied by a rare wine that cost thousands per bottle. Who knew she would have been content with a pizza from Domino's and a Diet Dr Pepper?

"Do you have any plans in the coming weeks?"

"Me? Plans?" She took a sip of her beverage. "I'll have to check my social calendar," she said, then grinned. "What did you have in mind?"

"I thought you might like a small vacation."

"Really? Where?"

"Let it be a surprise."

After lunch, Wade excused himself and returned to his office, saying he needed to make some phone calls.

Victoria walked with him partway; when he turned left down another corridor, she got onto the elevator. But instead of selecting the second floor, she leaned on the hold button. She didn't want to go back to her room; she wanted to be outside. The late-afternoon sun was still shining, and the memory of the tranquil blue-green water of the pool was a heady invitation. Without further thought, she stepped back out of the elevator and headed to the pool.

Towels were kept in a cabinet, along with sunscreen and sunglasses and a few other items. She grabbed one of the towels and walked to the edge of the enormous pool. It was shaped like a lagoon and was surrounded with tropical plants. The waterfall at the far end was too tempting. She quickly shed her blouse and jeans to reveal the yellow bikini underneath. Without testing the water, she dropped the towel on top of her clothes on a chair, moved to an area where the water was deeper and dived in. So cool and refreshing! She loved to swim. She loved the water. Both were things she hadn't considered yet. Maybe some of her memory was coming back.

She turned onto her back, partially floating, partially paddling the water with her hands, each stroke taking her closer to the falls. The giant boulders flanking each side had natural indentations where ivy and other cascading plants grew. The falls fell from a height of fifteen feet or more above the water and were just as wide.

She dived under the falls, came up on the other side and found herself at the opening of a huge cavern. The water gradually grew more shallow until she was walking up a wide set of stairs leading into an aboveground cave. The space would easily hold a dozen people. It had heavy wooden beams across the top and a skylight set into the center. There were reclining chairs, a sofa, a table for four and a small bar. It even had a large flat-screen television. The cave was made entirely of rock. The cream-colored floor was smooth alabaster laced with the brown color of the cave walls. Lit from beneath, it cast a soft glow over the space, giving it a feeling of solitude where the busy world could not break in. A fire pit lay ready and waiting, extending up from the center of the wide steps. She could hear soft music being piped in over the sound of the falling water.

It was amazing. Without any thought of *should she or shouldn't she?* Victoria climbed the four steps and stepped onto the translucent stone panels, which melded perfectly into the softly glowing floor. The bar top was made of the same smooth material and was the highlight of that area. She roamed around, amazed that from the outside, the hill covered in tropical plants and flowers was in fact a cover-up for a cavern complete with furniture and a big screen.

"What are you doing in here?" Wade's voice cut into the tranquility.

She spun around to face him. "I… Nothing. I was just looking around. This is incredible." She felt the blood drain from her face as she perceived this to be yet another area of this colossal house that was off-limits. Wade wasn't smiling.

He climbed the steps without seeming to move at

all, dressed in a pair of trunks that left very little to the imagination. Heat pooled in her lower abdomen, and her mouth became dry. The closer he got, the better she could see his expression. He didn't look angry so much as amazed. "More to the point, how did you get in here?"

"Through the falls. I don't know of another way in. Is there one?"

"What are you even doing in the pool?"

"Swimming. What, am I not allowed in here either? Is there a silent alarm here, too?" She could hear the frustration in her voice. She had reached her limit of being told where she could go and couldn't go, what she could and couldn't do.

"Victoria." He gripped her upper arms and gave her a small shake. "Dammit. You don't know how to swim!"

Seven

"Apparently I do," she replied. "Actually, I love the water. I think. And this grotto behind the falls is awesome. I've never seen anything like it—that I can remember. I didn't hurt or damage anything."

"It never occurred to me that you would. I was merely concerned for your safety." Still looking at her as though he didn't believe a word she said, he finally nodded his head and released her arms but refused to let her out of his sight. "I need a drink. What would you like?" he asked over his shoulder as he turned and walked to the bar. "I used to keep this pretty well stocked, but there hasn't been anyone using these facilities in a couple of years."

"Not even you when you are at home?"

"No time. What will you have?"

"I haven't got a clue."

"Okay, well, you used to like rosé, so let us find out." He walked over to a large wine rack and selected a bottle.

"This is Château d'Esclans 'Garrus' Rosé from Provence, France, 2010. They produce only six barrels per year. I was lucky." His fluent, near perfect French was seductive.

"How many languages do you speak?"

"Six. A seventh if you want to count just getting by. Why do you ask?"

Victoria shrugged. "Just curious. You speak French beautifully. It sounds sexy. I can't help but wonder if I speak other languages. Probably not."

She walked over to Wade and watched as he easily removed the cork and grabbed two wineglasses from the glass shelving behind them.

"I think we need a toast," Victoria said after he had poured each of them a glass of the sparkling rosé. "To your project in Belize. May it be amazing."

"I'd prefer a different toast. Here's to my wife not drowning today."

She laughed and touched her glass to his. "I'll definitely drink to that." She took her first sip. "Oh, my gosh, this is delicious!" she said as she swallowed another. "Oh, my gosh, Wade."

"Glad you still like it. It's what I usually prefer when I'm out here near the pool."

"Wade, I really do know how to swim." She was determined to make him believe her. "I enjoy doing so. Either you misunderstood me, or—"

"Or you lied to me before." He looked at her straight on, but she met his eyes without flinching.

"Why would I do that?"

"I don't have the slightest idea, but it happens. Quite often, actually." He sat down on the edge of the couch and turned to face her. "How did you know you could swim?"

"I don't know. I enjoyed the pool while you were in New York and wanted to come back. It's amazing." She took another sip of her wine. Was that why they weren't together? Did she get caught in a lie? Her instincts were screaming *no!*

"You do know that if you'd been wrong and couldn't swim, you would have been in trouble with no one around to help you."

She shrugged. "Maybe. But as soon as I got in the water, it felt okay."

Wade ran a hand across his lower face. "Victoria, I don't want you coming out here unless you have someone with you. Someone who knows how to swim."

"*I* know how to swim," she countered.

"Maybe. Maybe not."

Victoria set her glass on an end table. "How do you think I got here?"

"Probably because you can swim a little, but a percentage of that could have been luck."

Victoria knew what he was saying, and she felt her heart speed up because he apparently cared. "I appreciate the sentiments. I do. But I assure you nothing about me swimming to this grotto was luck. Why do you think I can't swim?"

"Because you've always been very nervous around the water. You told me you never learned to swim and didn't care to try. You avoided pool parties at all costs. You lived off Dramamine the few times I got you on board the yacht."

"We have a yacht?"

"The point is I don't want you taking unnecessary chances."

"I…" She didn't know what to say. She wouldn't have said such a thing to him, would she? Either he mistook something she said, or she had lied to Wade. According to Wade, lying was a common practice for her before her accident. That thought made her very uncomfortable.

"I'm going back to the house." Before he could try to stop her, she ran down the steps, dived into the deeper water under the falls and kept swimming. By the time Wade caught up with her, she was out of the pool and grabbing a towel.

"Victoria, wait," Wade called behind her. His request was ignored. She wanted to go back to the house. She needed to be alone. She had to have time to sort this out. What had happened between them? She didn't feel as though she was one who would lie to her husband, especially about something as trivial as knowing how to swim.

She scooted through the back door and headed down the hall toward the elevator and pushed the call button.

"Victoria, I need you to listen to me."

"Why? So you can accuse me of telling more lies?" She shook her head and glared at him. "You have the winning hand and refuse to give me a chance. Something is wrong between us. I felt it the day we came home from the hospital. If you won't tell me what happened, then I can do nothing to fix it." She pushed the button again. "If this is the way our marriage was, I don't care to continue. Two people who are married are supposed to love each other. I feel no love coming from you, Wade. Only brief glimpses of sympathy."

The door opened, and she stepped into the elevator. Unfortunately, Wade followed her inside.

"I won't stay in a house where I'm not wanted, and clearly that's the case. Give me a couple of days to make some arrangements, and I'll be out of your hair."

"Victoria, you can't leave."

She glared. "Do not tell me what I can and cannot do. Except for my memory, I'm perfectly healthy. Your obligation to bring me here until I healed is over. You won't have to look at me again or listen to any more lies."

She was mad, hurt, frustrated; all the emotions that had been building over the past two weeks had reached the surface. Nothing was ever going to change. To remain in a loveless marriage that had no hope of getting better was pointless. She didn't need her memory to know that.

"Victoria—"

She held up a hand indicating whatever he had to say she didn't want to hear. The elevator doors opened, and she quickly stepped into the hallway and beat a path for her room.

For the first time, she locked her door behind her. Wade knocked and was rewarded with a clear "Go away."

After a few more attempts, he must have left. Turning to the shower, she dropped her bathing suit and stepped under the spray. Where would she go? There must be women's shelters somewhere nearby. Maybe Roe could give her some ideas in the morning. She hated to involve Wade's staff, but she didn't know the answers. Maybe she could find the apartment Wade had mentioned she kept in Dallas? Unless he owned it. Oh, God, if only her memory would come back.

It had been almost a month. Surely Victoria should be getting her memory back by now. Wade was a man, and he knew she wanted him. She needed his body as badly as he needed hers. But she was holding out because she didn't know anything about their past. He'd considered many times not telling her the whole truth and just saying they had been about to divorce. Then they could work their way through their issues and become a couple. But no. When her memory came back, she would sure as hell know about their past, about the contract. And what actions would she bring in a lawsuit then? Why should he want them to be a couple? He'd never especially cared for her before the accident. He'd never been attracted to her the way he apparently was now. And when her memory returned, there was every likelihood she would revert to the snobbish woman she'd always been. This entire situation was driving him crazy.

What if he told her the truth? What if he told her about the contract? Would that appease her? Would Victoria then understand what kind of marriage this was and accept it? It might even serve to bring back some of her memories. Certainly he wanted her fully healthy. But telling Victoria the truth of their relationship could cause more consternation than she needed at this time in her recovery. Still, did he have an option? He was tired of the half-truths. Tired of kissing her, feeling her body respond to him and having to step away. He knew the time was coming when he wouldn't be able to stop. Each time he held her, it became more difficult to let go. At least if she knew the truth, she could make the decision knowing all the facts surrounding their relationship. Right now she thought he had stopped loving her. How convoluted was that? He'd only in recent weeks begun to see her in a light that could lead him to *start* loving her.

Dinner that evening was uncomfortable, and that was an understatement. Even so, the menu was amazing. The main course was filet mignon with white truffle risotto and Italian kimchi-style escarole with anchovies and Calabrian chilies. A dark red rosé accompanied the meal. It no doubt was delicious, but the food stuck in his throat. The coziness he'd previously felt in the new dining room was now oppressive. And it seemed that neither one of them had an appetite.

After a long, uncomfortable silence, he decided to address the elephant in the room. "Victoria, people get married for many different reasons. It's not always solely because of love."

"Are you saying ours was like a marriage of convenience? Or…or…did I get pregnant?"

"No, you didn't get pregnant. I wish you would just let it go. What was in the past is in the past. Can we not go forward?"

"Forward to where? How can I go forward if I don't know where I've been?"

For a long minute neither moved.

"Come on." He stood up. "Walk with me."

He guided her back toward the elevator. When the doors opened, he accompanied her inside and pushed the button for the second floor. Rather than taking her to her room, they went farther down the hall to his. When they were inside, he indicated for her to sit. She chose one of the chairs near the fireplace. He pulled up a chair and sat down facing her.

He rubbed the back of his neck. "I agree that keeping the past from you isn't fair. You have the right to know. Then you can make your own decision whether you want to stay or go. But I won't try to stop you."

"Why at times do I get the feeling you hate me?"

He ground his teeth.

"I don't hate you, Victoria."

"Try again. It's like sometimes you want to hold me

and make love to me. I feel your desire. I know it. I can tell. Then you push me away, or you walk away like it would be a bad thing. I…I don't know what I did that was so bad. You claimed that I often lied to you. About what? How am I ever going to make amends if you don't tell me what it is? I need to know, Wade. Like, about the water. Why would I lie about something so simple? What could possibly be my motivation?"

She gazed into his eyes. The golden flecks in his brown eyes seemed to glow in the ambient lighting. His masterful lips were held in a straight line, but she couldn't tear her eyes away.

He released a deep breath. "It's complicated, Victoria. Until your memory returns, I don't know how much you will understand."

"That's unfair." She looked at him. "You're holding something against me that I can't apologize for. I can't make it right because I don't know what it is that I did. I want to know about us." She stared into his face, not willing to look away or offer him the same option. "I want to know the truth. Since the day I woke up in the hospital after the wreck, I've never seen anything more in your eyes than sympathy and, on occasion, the glimmer of arousal, which you effectively snub out. You can give compassion to a homeless person. You can hire a woman if you need sexual release. I want to know why I'm here. Are we honestly even married?"

Wade hesitated to the point she didn't think he was going to answer. "Yes. We are married."

To her horror, tears sprang into her eyes and fell down her cheeks. "Did I have an affair? Is that it? Was that why you got so angry the first day I was here? Because I asked about Murphy? I can tell you I wasn't thinking of any particular man when I asked about that name."

Wade merely looked at her.

"That's it, isn't it? There was another man." She felt sick. How could there have been anyone else in her life when she had Wade?

"No. Yes. I honestly don't know." He gritted his teeth, his jaw muscles working overtime. "It might be rumor. You are the only one who can answer that, and you can't until your memory returns."

"Oh, that's a great answer. I've lain in bed and tried to imagine what I did that would alienate my husband so completely, but I have no clue. If it's in my head, it won't come out."

"Victoria…"

Her voice was broken. "You're my husband. I love you. But I can't go on like this."

He closed the bedroom door as he watched her closely in the ambient light.

She took a deep breath. "What came between us?"

For several minutes she didn't think he was going to answer. Then he turned toward her, sat back down in the chair and clasped his hands together between his knees.

"Some people say I'm a workaholic. They're probably right. I'm used to traveling, setting priorities and making things happen. I spend more time en route than

I do here or anywhere in the United States. Therefore, I'm not good husband material. I realized years ago that CEOs of other companies tended to work better with those who were married, who had a stable home and a family environment. I don't know why, but there it is. Business tends to go better if I give the impression I'm an established family man."

He paused to look at her as if trying to tell if he was making any sense. "There were past relationships. They went badly. I'd rather not go into the details, but marriage to a loving bride was not going to happen for me. Let's just say I have…trust issues."

He rubbed the back of his neck. "And you? You wanted to be in the inner circles of the elite rich. After your father lost all of his money…well, you were devastated. So, we made a bargain. A written contract. You would become my wife on paper only for a period of one year. If we both were in agreement at the end of the year, if we both met the contractual stipulations, we had the option of renewing it. If you bailed out before the year was over, you would forfeit a million dollars. There are other stipulations. Either of us, for instance, could see others as long as we were discreet and it didn't go public. There were other things involved in the agreement, but that's basically it.

"If I made love to you, I'd feel like I was taking advantage of you. It wouldn't be fair until you knew about the agreement. I couldn't do that." He shook his head. "I've tried to leave you alone, but since you came home from the hospital, there's something…something

I can't ignore. My apologies for almost letting it get out of hand."

Victoria was in shock. She didn't know what to say. Of all the things she had imagined, it was as far as you could get from this. A contract. His statement explained so much. He didn't love her. He didn't have to love her. He needed only to be cordial and ensure she was made comfortable until the end of the agreement. During that time he would continue to travel, immerse himself in his business matters and leave her in this place alone. A searing pain pierced her heart.

"So…we're really married."

"On paper only."

"And you don't or never did love me?" It hurt to ask the question, but she had to know.

The answer was a long time coming. "No."

The tears welled in her eyes and fell down her cheeks. She felt humiliated. Hurt. A fool.

"I should definitely go." She sniffed and grabbed a tissue from the table by the bed. "If there is a suitcase I can borrow, I would appreciate it until I get settled."

"Go? Victoria, I don't want you to go."

"No, I guess you don't. How would you ever be the settled family man if I left?" She sucked in a deep breath. "Come on, save yourself a million, and just lend me the suitcase. I can't live like this. I don't know anyone who could. Of course, I don't know many people right now." She tried to insert a bit of humor, but it failed miserably. She kept wiping her face, but the tears kept coming. "I must have been out of my mind to ever agree to such a thing." She walked to the door, but Wade beat her to it. Still wiping the tears that ran nonstop, she stood in front of the closed door and waited with more patience than she felt for him to open it. "I'm sorry about the amnesia thing. It must have really put a crimp in your plans."

"Victoria."

"No, Wade. No more. I don't need details. You've told me everything I need to know. I just want a suitcase and a taxi that can take me…somewhere."

He stood looking down at her for the longest time.

"I would like to leave now." He opened the door and she walked through. Somehow Victoria made it to her room and to the bed before the dam burst. She cried hard, tears of hopelessness and deep sorrow. Tears that came from her heart. What a fool she'd made of herself. She thought back on all the worry about not fitting in with Wade, his world, his lifestyle. At least now she knew why. She had to wonder if she ever had fit in. She glanced down at the silver ring on her left hand. With its assorted stones, it was gaudy and too big. She slid it off her finger and put it in a drawer. It was so not her and it didn't represent the caring admiration a real husband was supposed to have for his wife. As she closed the drawer, more tears welled in her eyes. This was a nightmare. A lurid dream from which she couldn't seem to awaken.

What in hell was he thinking? He had finally admitted the nature of their relationship, and she'd taken it a lot harder than he would have expected. He couldn't believe the truth had rolled out of his mouth. When he'd heard the words, it sounded unbelievable even to himself. It sounded cold and calculating, which of course it was. Victoria's reaction tonight was far from her smile of elation when he'd first presented the idea. She'd gone after it tooth and nail. Couldn't wait to sign on the dotted line. Couldn't wait to move into the mansion. And certainly couldn't wait to begin living the high life.

Wade felt bad about it. He couldn't think he'd done the wrong thing in telling her. She deserved to know. It was a situation of damned if he did, damned if he didn't. But he hadn't expected her to immediately want to leave. He didn't want her to leave, especially since there was no place safe she could go. She would require a bodyguard. She probably didn't remember that and he had a feeling this new Victoria would not be thrilled by that fact. Sadly, that was what his life had come down to when he wasn't at the ranch. He had a feeling that convincing her of this would be next to impossible, which would only lead to more anger and frustration.

But fearing for her safety from kidnapping was not the only reason he wanted her to stay. She had changed. She intrigued him. If their situation were different, he would have already invited this new version of Victoria out, and by now would have had her in his bed. The problem with that train of thought was he didn't want it to be a onetime thing. He wanted more from Victoria than a couple of nights in bed. He wanted to continue getting to know her. She was smart, beautiful and sexy as hell. And she wasn't trying to be any of those things, which made her even sexier. She had an air of innocence about her. Fresh and vivacious, she touched him on more levels than anyone he'd ever known. While he'd not spent time analyzing his feelings, he knew what he felt for Victoria was different from anything he'd experienced with any other woman. It was exciting and new. It was also frightening in that when her memory returned, it was possible she would revert to the way she used to be. She'd become as different as night and day from her old self, and while he wanted her to regain her memory, he desperately hoped her personality wouldn't revert to the way she had been. He'd always envied his brothers for finding the perfect women, while at the same time telling himself he had the perfect life. No complications. Just doing what he loved and what he was very good at: finance. Corporate mergers. Contracts.

He actually had never given any thought to truly settling down and having a family. Until recently. What Victoria would do when her memory returned and how much she and her mother would try to milk him for were suddenly number one on the I Don't Give a Shit list. But that thought twisted into the fact that he desperately didn't want her to become her old self again. He was walking a tightrope between desire and reality and it was making him crazy.

A little voice reminded him of all the lies and the fact that Victoria couldn't be trusted. All the men she had supposedly been with over the past few months alone. Then there was the question of whether it was all a setup. Something staged to make him jealous or for some other nefarious act to provide her with more money. *That* he honestly didn't know.

He paced the floor, needing to find a resolution. Maybe after she'd had a chance to calm down, they could talk. Maybe after he'd had a chance to think, he would see the current situation a lot differently. Right now he felt as though he'd just found her, and tomorrow, if he left it up to her, she would be gone. He would not permit it. Muttering under his breath, he walked to the shower. How had he managed to get himself into such a damnable situation?

Deep down where no one could see, he'd started having illusions of becoming the family man that up until now had just been an irritating thought. Since the accident, Victoria had brought to light how lonely life really was. Oh, there was plenty of socializing, parties on the yacht, dinners at the finest restaurants around the world. If he needed to, he could always find a date with women who knew how to play the game.

But there was no comparing them to Victoria. For the first time, he was beginning to glimpse his solitary, structured life through her eyes. It *was* an empty, often lonely existence. It was a life without nurturing, consisting of accomplishments no one cared about, other than those who would benefit monetarily. Over the past weeks, he had fought against these ridiculous sentiments, but he couldn't deny the way he felt when he and Victoria were together: alive and looking forward to the next day. There was no posturing, no expectations other than to just be himself. At times it felt as though an enormous weight had been lifted. Still, Wade held on to caution.

Because when her memory returned, the old Victoria would be back. He knew it in his heart.

Eight

A knock on the door broke the silence of the night. Victoria turned from the window where she'd been staring out at the garden below. Unable to sleep, she'd paced at first, then started packing a few clothes to take with her when she left. She wouldn't take much because Wade had probably bought most of it for her. When she was done, she'd soaked in the tub, which helped a little to settle her nerves. Then she'd put on a nightgown and gone to the balcony.

She looked at the clock. It was three in the morning. There could be only one person knocking at her door at this time of night.

Finally, the door opened. Wade stood on the threshold, tall and muscled, wearing only a pair of sweats.

"I just wanted to check on you." He ran a hand through his hair; it appeared as though it wasn't the first time he'd done so tonight. "I know I upset you, and that wasn't my intention."

Victoria shrugged. "It is what it is. At least now I understand a lot of things that didn't make any sense before. I'm fine. At least I will be as soon as I can find my own place."

"Victoria, I don't want you to go. It's not safe for you to be out in the world without your memory intact. I don't want you to leave, period."

"Wade…you've shown me kindness by bringing me here and caring for me when I had no place else to go. I can now repay you by breaking that contract. You shouldn't have to be out any more money because of me."

"I don't give a damn about the money." He took in a deep breath and blew it out. "I'm worried about you. We've known each other for almost five years as casual acquaintances. Until the accident, I never really knew you at all. The relationship we have now is different than before. We've gotten to know each other this time. I like having you here. I want to know you better. I'd hoped you might still want to stay here and get to know me after learning the truth of our relationship."

She looked up at him. Was he seriously asking her to stay? "Would a clothing-store mannequin not work as well for you? No feelings, no emotions to have to deal with, just give her a name and there you go. She won't break any rules and I can guarantee she won't be calling out other men's names when you are in her presence. She might have a hard time signing a new contract, but what the hell. You can sign it yourself."

She moved to close the door, but Wade blocked it.

"Victoria."

She loved him. In the short time they'd had together that she could remember, she had fallen in love with this incredibly complex man. But her heart was breaking. All this time, she'd been afraid she'd done something wrong, and he'd let her go on thinking it. She could now add anger to the feelings of frustration and guilt.

"What exactly do you want from me now? I don't have anything else to give."

"Let's see where this goes, Victoria. You might find you want nothing to do with me—"

"Ya think?"

"—but I would like to give it a chance. We have almost two months until the contract is up."

"Oh, okay, let's put it on a timer. See if you can fall in love with your wife in two months. Got a stopwatch?" Her sarcasm was not lost on Wade.

"Dammit, Victoria." Wade closed the door behind him, grasped her shoulders and gently pushed her against the nearby wall. "That's not what I meant. I didn't expect to have these feelings for you when this whole thing started. And I didn't expect you to feel anything for me. You didn't, you know…when we made up the contract. You just wanted money and prestige. I'm sorry for not telling you before now, but it was a two-way street."

It had never occurred to her that she'd wanted the contract as much as he did. Since being discharged from the hospital, they'd both begun to respond to the magnetic pull between them until they were unable to deny the intensity of love growing there. Those emotions trumped a contract as far as she was concerned. She nodded her head.

No matter what else happened in her life, she knew that in his arms was where she wanted to be. Not for money or prestige. Just to be held close and wanted like any woman who was in love with her husband.

He lowered his face to hers so that they were inches apart. Gently he wiped the tears from her eyes. "I want to explore the possibility that we have something special. I want you to be more than a token wife. I want you to give us a chance."

She didn't think she could cry any more, but in that she was wrong. Tears of happiness welled in her eyes. "No more withholding the truth. No more remote politeness. Oh, I'm so tired of being treated like a guest in my own home. Or rather, in your home."

"*Our* home."

"I don't want your money. Promise me that contract will be torn to shreds either way."

"We can discuss it later." One large hand came to rest on her shoulder. "Much later." He placed two fingers under her chin and tilted her head to meet his gaze. "Stay, Victoria. Stay here with me."

The dam broke, and Wade kissed her hard. He drew her to him, and as soon as she responded to him, the kiss deepened. He'd kissed her before since returning from the hospital, but this was different. There was no hesitation, no uncertainty. No right or wrong. It was as though she was his, and he intended to show her exactly what that meant. All barriers were down.

He scooped her into his arms and walked out the door and down the hall to his suite. He threw back the covers and gently placed her on the bed. The soft lighting shone on the muscles of his arms, his broad chest and tight abs. He stepped out of his pants and followed her down, kissing her in long, lingering exchanges.

"You're my wife, Victoria. And you're going to be in every way that matters," he said roughly as he pushed away the straps of her nightgown. "In my bed is where you need to be. If you don't want me, tell me now."

For several long moments she held his gaze. In the ambient light she could see his eyes as they roamed over her face. Then she raised her head and placed her lips on his. He pressed her down on the mattress, and her arms went around his neck.

"I don't think I've ever wanted anything more in my life," she whispered. With that, he kissed her again, more deeply, like he couldn't get enough of her.

He held her tightly, as though forgetting his strength, but it only served to make her heart beat faster with excitement. She'd wondered what it would be like to make love to him without all the restraints he had kept in place when he'd kissed her before. She was about to find out. She wanted to melt into him. She opened to the demands of his lips and tongue.

Without lifting his head, he shifted her to the center of the bed, working his knee between her legs to part them. His body pressed her down into the pliable softness of the mattress. He brushed her hair back away from her face and kissed down her neck, nipping at her collarbone, licking her ear before moving to her breasts. He eased her nightgown all the way off, and his hands covered the velvet softness of her breasts, causing the nipples to go taut. Her back arched up in a natural response, and she moaned.

"What do you want, Victoria?"

She let go of his shoulder and found his hands with hers, causing him to press her nipples more firmly. She heard him chuckle softly.

"Is this what you need?"

He bent his head and sucked a rosy tip into his mouth. She couldn't forestall a moan as he suckled the nipple, hard. She grabbed his hair, holding him to her. Then he changed to the other breast, giving it the same attention. Growling, he returned to her lips and kissed her long and deep.

Wade left her mouth and began a trail of kisses down her abdomen, to the sweet spot between her legs.

"Open for me?" His voice was low, guttural. Victoria complied. His large hands spread her knees farther apart, and he put his mouth and tongue to work.

"Oh..." she cried out in rapture, never having felt anything like this in her life. Surely she would know if she had. How could she forget this glorious feeling? Finding her special spot, Wade alternately teased it with his tongue and suckled. Suddenly everything went still. Seconds later she exploded, her body quivering in a delight that was indescribable. Wade laid his head on her stomach and held her until the tremors had passed. Victoria was limp, satiated. But Wade wasn't finished.

He spread her legs wide again. Then he began to taste every inch of her again. Her nipples were erect, and he sucked them hard, using his tongue to circle and lick the rosy buds.

She felt his shaft press against her core and violent shivers raced down her spine, centering between her legs. Her hands raked at the smooth muscles of his back, silently asking for more. She heard a soft moan and realized it came from her own throat. Wade returned to her mouth, drinking deep, lapping at her tongue. Victoria couldn't get enough of him, her body's natural instincts responding to his every move.

Her fingers corded through the thickness of his hair. She pushed against him, knowing he was the only one who could quench the fire that blazed out of control deep within her.

"I can't hold off any longer." His baritone voice was rough and laced with passion. "I need to be in you." His powerful body was trembling with need.

"Yes," she murmured against his lips. The male scent of him surrounded her. His lips were so hungry, kissing her over and over while his erection pressed against her center. His hand moved down her body to her core, testing her wetness, making sure she was ready for him. Then using his hand to guide his shaft, he pushed inside. Victoria drew in a sharp, deep breath and tensed. Wade came to an immediate stop, realizing he'd met resistance.

His heart was beating hard against the wall of his chest as he held himself still.

"Victoria…"

His upper body trembled as he fought to lift himself from her and bring all activity to a halt.

"Wade, what's wrong?"

He pushed against her inner core again, and again she cried out in discomfort.

"You're a virgin." He shook his head, unable to believe it. It was impossible.

His head swam. How was it possible that Victoria had never been with a man? Her various dalliances had made the headlines. But still, there was no getting around the reality of the situation, surreal as it was.

"Hon, if you've never been with a man, this may hurt."

"I don't care." She pressed her lips to his, hungry for whatever he could give to make the need stop.

"God, Victoria," he murmured against her lips. "Are you sure you want this?"

"Yes," she whispered. "I love you, Wade."

He cupped her face and stared into her eyes. Then lowering his head, he sought her lips before moving to her neck. Taking tender bites along the sensitive cord, he whispered into her ear, "Are you ready for me, Victoria?"

She nodded, breathing fast. Pushing deep inside, he felt the barrier give, and it was done. He held perfectly still, waiting for a signal from Victoria that she wanted to continue.

She began to bestow kisses on his neck and throat, taking small bites, her hands raking his broad shoulders as she silently gave him her answer. He couldn't hold himself back any longer and began to move. With each push, each movement, the pressure once again began to build. Only now the pressure was different. Heat was building to a scorching level.

He couldn't get close enough, couldn't get deep enough as she returned his kisses.

"Oh, Wade," she called out.

He stopped as the perspiration broke out on his face. "Are you all right?" he said against her mouth, then rained kisses over her neck and ear.

Victoria managed to nod her head. "Don't stop."

Then he began to move once again. He grasped her hip with one hand, raising her to him, and the world tilted on its axis. Wade could sense the moment was near; the heat was reaching an all-time high.

"Come for me, babe," Wade growled in her ear, and she cried out. Wade soon joined her, reaching an outrageously intense climax of his own. She held him tight, kissing the moist skin of his face and neck.

Wade dropped onto the mattress next to her, pulling her close, still breathing hard. He gently turned her face to his and kissed her again. Time seemed to stop and the world outside disappeared.

The scent of sex and luscious female enveloped

him as Wade lay next to her, his leg over hers, his arm around her. Together they fell asleep.

Sometime later, Wade awakened her with soft kisses. "Sweetheart, you're moaning in your sleep. Let's get you in a warm bath. It will help you feel better."

She nodded her head, her body still boneless from the lovemaking.

Wade had already drawn a bath. He gently lowered her into the tub and followed her in, situating himself behind her. He adjusted the jets of water, and she relaxed against him. He loved the silkiness of her skin, loved the feeling of her hair against his neck. Loved the feel of her.

Later in the night, Wade came to her again. He woke her with kisses down her shoulder and back until she turned to him, and his lips once again covered hers. This time was better than the first. She was hungry for him and met him touch for touch, breath for breath. The ending was a blazing trail to the stars, and cuddled together, they drifted back to sleep.

Wade began the next morning by offering to give her a tour of his downtown Dallas offices. His building was twenty stories high, all dark glass and concrete. She met so many nice people. His office, like everything else in his world, was extreme, taking up almost half of the top floor. The walls and massive executive desk were mahogany, and the floor-to-ceiling windows offered a panoramic view of the rapidly expanding city. Attached to his office was a room almost as large for the administrative staff and yet another with a conference table that would probably seat twenty people. He had a language center with employees who handled overseas calls. A personal bathroom and spa. The list of amenities went on.

"You could almost live here," she laughed.

"Sometimes I do." He had no smile on his face when he said it. "Ready to go?"

Wade approached where she sat. She couldn't help but feel a new hope. A huge weight had been lifted. And the promise of a new future had begun.

She nodded and, with Wade beside her, walked to the elevators and went down to the lobby and out into the sunshine.

"What would you think about taking a vacation?" he asked once they were seated in the limo. "You seem to like nature and the great outdoors."

"Sounds tempting."

"I know of a place that's just what the doctor ordered. Pun intended, but he did say you should be fine if we relocated for a while."

"I'm more than okay with that. Where is it you had in mind?"

Wade shook his head. "Wait and see. We won't be leaving the country. I'm not fully convinced you're up to that. But it's a place I hope you'll like."

"Okay." She smiled and shrugged. Why not? It had to be better than the big house in the city. And after his confession last night, she was beginning to get used to the idea of trusting her husband. "When do we leave?"

"In the morning. Dress casual. Jeans would be great."

Jeans. She could handle jeans.

It seemed that Wade was full of surprises. The next morning it was a short drive to a small airport where the Masters family's planes were housed. They drove to the end of a hangar where a dark blue helicopter with Masters International painted in silver letters on the side waited, the rotor blades already churning.

"Are you kidding me?"

"Come on," he said, smiling, no doubt at how her jaw had dropped.

Reluctantly she accepted Wade's hand and got out of the car. The wind from the helicopter blades whipped her hair around her face. She held fast to his hand as they approached the chopper. He opened the door, indicating she should slide into the back seat. Then he closed her door before going to the other side and climbing in beside her. The first thing he did was hand her a set of earphones with a microphone attached. Putting on a headset of his own, he told her to buckle up and closed his door.

"Ready?"

"No." She glanced around the cozy interior. "And don't try to convince me I've done this before."

"You're a natural." He pursed his lips, a wicked glint showing in his eyes.

"At what?"

Wade laughed and gave the pilot a thumbs-up. The man opened the throttle, increasing the speed of the main rotor. The sound of the engine grew louder as the blades spun faster and faster. It was exhilarating and scary at the same time. After a few seconds, the chopper lifted off the helipad, momentarily plunging forward before rising, and they were on their way. Victoria couldn't help but marvel at the sight out her window as they climbed high above the city skyline and headed east. Roads became ant trails, and cars the ants. She felt as light as a bird, and any initial fear quickly turned to exhilaration.

After circling the downtown Dallas area, they headed north. The city gave way to beautiful suburban homes and finally to the sprawling ranch lands of North Texas.

After about an hour Wade announced, "We're here." They began descending into a clearing amid a heavily forested area. The trees began to separate, showing green pastureland and several structures. The circular landing pad came into view some distance from what appeared to be a barn. On a small plateau, an area surrounded by white pipe fencing stretched almost out of sight. Both horses and cattle grazed in the abundant grass within the boundaries.

The pilot gently set the chopper down in the center of the remote helipad and killed the motor. Wade opened his door and got out first, then helped Victoria to the ground. Taking her hand, he guided her to a well-worn path that led into the trees, up a small rise to a huge log home faced with glass walls.

"How beautiful," she said as she pulled him to a stop to take in the beauty all around her. "This is where you grew up?"

He nodded. "Dad built this house when I was about six. Before that we lived three miles to the south in a smaller house. When Chance was born, it quickly became obvious larger digs were needed. It was a good place to grow up."

"Chance is your brother?"

"Yeah. He's the youngest. He and his wife, Holly, live here on the ranch. Chance manages, while Holly has a veterinarian practice across the road from the main house."

Victoria could hear the wistfulness in his voice and knew she wasn't imagining it. To Wade, this place was home. It was where he and his brothers had learned about life. Where Wade had grown into the man he had become today. This ranch was a part of his heart that could never be chipped away or taken from him. The fact that he wanted to share it with her made her almost giddy with happiness.

As they stepped onto the large front porch, the door was pulled open and a small whirlwind of a woman with blond hair raced toward Wade, not pausing until, with a jump, she was in his arms, welcoming him with a huge hug. They both laughed as Wade spun around.

"I couldn't believe it when they told me you were coming," she said with excitement. "It's so good to see you again!"

Wade set her on the deck, grinning broadly. "Holly, I want you to meet my wife. This is Victoria."

Her beautiful face still full of smiles, she didn't hesitate to welcome Victoria to both the ranch and to the family. "Wade Masters! You sure took your time bringing her out here. Oh, my gosh!" She laughed and, stepping over, gave Victoria a hug. "It's nice to meet you," she said with honest enthusiasm. She glanced back at Wade. "She's beautiful." She nudged his shoulder with her own. "You did *good*, dude."

"Victoria, this is Holly." Wade made the introductions. "Like I told you, her husband, Chance, manages the operation here. Holly grew up on the ranch. Her father was the previous manager. And this *brat* has been a thorn in my side for…twenty-three years?"

"Twenty-four next month," she corrected, a bit of pride in her voice. "Y'all come on in and make yourselves at home." She pushed open the heavy door and stepped aside, indicating they should precede her. "No one's been here since last August when Wade stopped by for a few days. I had Ms. Hughes give the house a good once-over to address the dust, freshen the linens. There's food in the pantry, steaks in the freezer, wine in the cellar… I think that's it. But if you need anything else, you know to call the office."

"Thanks, Holly. I appreciate it." Wade looked around and seemed to relax.

"No worries." Holly turned toward the door, stopping just inside. "Chance should be back on Wednesday. I hope you both will still be here then."

"That is the plan unless I get a call. You know how that goes."

"Good deal. I gotta scoot. Later!"

"She's a special person," Victoria commented when Holly had gone.

Wade nodded. "Honestly, I had some concerns about her when Chance first enlisted in the military. She loved him even back then as a teenager. Saying goodbye was hard on all of us, but especially Holly. But she's tough. Chance ended up a Navy SEAL. I didn't think anything or anyone could inspire him to give up that life. Holly did it. I don't think she really ever asked him to leave the navy, she just made Chance realize how much she loved him and what he was giving up here."

Victoria nodded her understanding. Obviously Holly thought of Wade as an older brother, which said a lot about Wade. She had a feeling this was going to be an eye-opening visit in a number of ways.

She took in her surroundings. It was a magnificent home. Large but cozy, with walls of split log and drywall, a thirty-foot-high ceiling and a huge stone fireplace with a hand-carved mantel. Massive overhead beams ran the length of the ceiling and the tall glass panes gave a view of the valley that was to die for. The kitchen featured a large island with hickory cabinets and granite countertops. A polished hardwood floor finished off the design scheme. "This house is fantastic. I love it. Thank you for bringing me here."

"There are four bedrooms and a master suite upstairs. Our luggage will be taken there if you have no objections."

They would be sharing a room? She grinned. "No problem here."

Wade leaned over and kissed her. "Someone will bring our luggage in a little while. Are you hungry?"

"No. Not at all." They'd had a light breakfast before they left. "I want to see your ranch."

That earned her a raised eyebrow, tipped head and curious look from her husband. He shrugged. "Say no more. The ranch we will see. At least part of it."

Wade led the way outside to a storage unit also made of logs and mortar at the rear of the house. He opened the double doors, revealing several four-wheelers parked inside.

"The best way to see anything on a ranch this size is an ATV." He turned toward her. "Ever ridden one before?"

All she could do was shrug. "Not that I remember. But I'm willing to give it a shot."

"Let's not take a chance. How about you ride with me for your first outing?"

Wade swung his leg over a red ATV. Revving up the engine, he nodded to her to climb on behind him and handed her a helmet. Her arms went around his waist, and she felt the tight abdominal muscles beneath her fingers.

With two revs and a squeal from Victoria, they were off. She couldn't hold back another scream as they topped a rise and plunged down the other side.

"Slow down!" she called out, laughing. She was holding on to him so tight she probably fractured one of his ribs, but Wade didn't seem to mind. He was a big, incredibly fit man, and her arms barely reached entirely around his waist.

He nodded his head, indicating he'd heard her request to slow up. But instead, he gave it some gas, and they shot forward. They hit rises that took them off the ground, skirted holes in the turf and drove full speed up and over mounds of dirt, with Victoria screaming and laughing the whole way.

The first stop was the main barn. Victoria quickly got off the four-wheeler, swearing she would never get back on the thing. "You're a maniac!" Wade actually laughed out loud.

Most of the stalls were full, and the horses inside them looked amazing. She hurried to one, a beautiful black-and-white paint.

"Wade." She looked back to make sure he was behind her. "She's beautiful. I've never seen anything like her. Well, that I can remember."

He stepped up beside her. "She's a Tobiano paint Tennessee Walker. As you can see, she's basically white with black patches on the body and legs. Some have dark brown, bay or chestnut patches. Most paints are Overo, which is a black or brown body with white patches. Some, like her, have a two-toned mane and tail and a dark face with a star and a snip or a wide blaze."

"She's amazing."

"My grandfather was concerned about this breed slowly being integrated with horses of solid color. If no one stepped up, we could have lost the DNA that produces these amazing markings. Thankfully several ranchers joined in, and they turned it around. Dad started a small herd years ago. I think today we maintain about thirty for our own use, including breeding stock."

With her long multicolored mane and tail and intricate patchwork of black against the white body, the horse was breathtakingly beautiful.

"Over here is a roan or, specifically, an Appaloosa." Wade moved down to the next stall. "They are also known for their odd markings. Most common is dark brown legs, mane, tail and lower body. Then they have a white blanket on their rear with tiny brown spots inside. This pattern is typical, but some are white with small brown or black spots covering the body, neck and legs."

"Sounds like you're describing a dalmatian."

Wade smiled. "That's what many look like. Often they have bold, clearly defined stripes on their hooves. Their temperament, endurance and versatility make them very popular. The Appaloosa and the Quarter Horse, more than any other breeds, helped make the West what it is."

They continued down the long aisle, Wade answering questions, and Victoria bubbling with excitement as stall after stall housed a horse that was beautiful and unique.

She felt as though she was staying at a Western resort. As they walked together down the center of a barn that had to house a hundred horses, Victoria couldn't take it all in. Every breath contained the scent of freshly baled hay, cedar shavings and leather.

"Most of the horses on the ranch are Quarter Horses," he explained. "You might see an Arabian or two and, of course, the Walkers. We breed and train the Quarter Horses and sell them to other ranches for work or recreation." She watched as Wade looked around the huge structure with wonder in his eyes just like hers.

From the massive barn, they ventured to the foal paddock, where the newborns were just finding their legs.

"We keep the mothers and their babies in this area for the first few weeks, just to make certain everything is okay. Then they are turned out into the general pasture until the foals are six months old and it's time to wean them."

"They are so adorable." The foals followed their mothers as they grazed. "It looks like they're all legs."

Wade chuckled, a sound she loved. "At this age, that's just about what they are. But they'll grow fast."

"When do you start to train them?"

"Already started. As soon as they are born, they are fitted with a halter and taught it's okay to feel pressure against their heads. By the time they enter this pasture, most can be led around. At six months, groundwork starts. They are trained to become used to someone handling them, brushing them, giving them baths. But they don't feel a saddle until they are about two. At three they carry their first rider, and an entirely new training begins."

Victoria didn't know how long they stood watching the foals—their antics were so fascinating. Finally, Wade called it a day.

"It's getting late. You must be hungry. Let's head back. We can saddle up a couple of horses tomorrow, if you like, and I'll show you more of the ranch."

"Sounds like a plan." She smiled and walked side by side with Wade out of the barn.

Nine

Wade was amazed. So far, Victoria hadn't made any negative comments since they'd first gotten in the chopper and headed to the ranch. He figured, when she realized the cabin was remote, she would find a bone to pick with that, but she hadn't said a word. She had even seemed to really enjoy looking at the horses. He just couldn't figure it out. None of this was typical Victoria behavior. Inside he was glad. Especially after what they'd shared. But at the same time, he remained cautious. None of it made any sense. It was the same twist-tie emotion he'd had since bringing her home from the hospital. He expected the worst but relished the feeling of delight when her behavior was nothing like what he'd anticipated.

Tomorrow they would head up to Stockman's Ridge. The only way to get there was on horseback. There were some really scenic views, but it was a tough ride. They should get back before the sun disappeared to attend the campfire. They'd sit on a log, eating red beans and sausage cooked over an open fire with some corn bread. As a kid it had been one of his favorite meals. No French chef, no expensive wine. And the only music was if one of the ranch hands brought his guitar.

If Victoria survived tomorrow, he was going to give up watching for inconsistencies in her behavior and just accept that she had amnesia and wasn't faking it. He had to accept it. Short of having her muck stalls, there was not a lot else he could do to bring out her true colors. If it turned out she really did love the ranch and the horses, he would enjoy every minute he was with her until her memory did truly return. If she changed at that time, he would face and deal with it then.

He certainly had never expected, with all the men she'd paraded around, that she would be a virgin. He'd almost lost it that night. No, Victoria wasn't at all what he expected when he brought her home from the hospital. And he thanked his lucky stars for that. If she truly did love the outdoors as much as he did, it was a match made in heaven. And that he was hard-pressed to believe. He must always remain aware that this was, in fact, Victoria. Her memory could come back at any time and bring with it the return of her old self as she was before the accident. A tinge of sadness touched his

heart. Would there ever be a time he could believe she
was who she presented herself to be?

When they returned to Pine House, a member of the
household staff told them their bags had been left in the
upstairs hallway outside the master bedroom. She ran
up the stairs, curious to see what it looked like. The
room was very spacious, with a large bed in the center draped in silk and printed with images of deer and
the forest. Across from the door a balcony beckoned.
Pushing the heavy drapes aside, she pulled open the
French doors. Below her was the barn, with pastures
and trees surrounding it as far as she could see. In the
distance she spotted a river with bright blue water. The
whole setting was breathtaking. How could Wade not
want to live here?

Dinner that night was around a campfire. About
twenty of the ranch hands joined them, digging into the
red beans, sausage and corn bread. She took her plate,
fork and napkin and found a seat on a huge overturned
tree trunk. Wade soon joined her. The ranch hands ran
the conversation, and Victoria was content to sit, eat and
listen. Talk about some tall tales. Most were hilarious
stories, and many involved Wade and his brothers as
kids. She laughed and ate until she felt she would pop.

She glanced at Wade, who sat back with his hat
pulled low over his face, listening to the stories, occasionally denying he had any part in the mischief being
described. This would cause the guys to all boo good-
naturedly. There was nothing arrogant or snobbish about
Wade. He'd known many of them most of his life, and

it appeared they liked him just like they would one of their own. *He should be here*, she thought. This was his home.

She realized she was looking at a completely different man from the one who lived in Dallas. Rather than having a forced smile on his face, this Wade sat back, totally contented and happy. He seemed to speak more freely and had an overall laid-back demeanor.

As the group began to break up, Wade and Victoria walked back to the house. "Did you want anything to keep by the bed in case you get thirsty tonight? Water? Tea? The housekeeper has the night off."

"No, thank you. I'm fine."

"Which side do you want?" Wade asked as they entered the suite.

"It doesn't matter to me. You pick."

She grabbed her nightgown and headed for the shower. Soon she was standing under the water, the warm spray enveloping her. The thought of sleeping with Wade that evening had her heart pumping. Wanting to be with him was turning into a craving so deep it almost hurt.

After a quick shower, she brushed her teeth and applied facial cream before brushing out her long hair. The flesh-colored silk nightgown clung to her curves, from her breasts to her hips. She opened the door and gazed out into the suite. It was dark. She could just make out the bed and the large figure on the far side of it.

She quietly padded to the free side of the bed, lifted the covers and climbed in. The mattress was indented from his weight, causing her to roll in that direction. Turning away, she wiggled until she could catch a hold of her side of the mattress and scoot herself over. This was a heck of a thing. If she let go, she would slide back against Wade.

"You can't possibly sleep holding on to the side of the mattress." Wade's deep voice carried a bit of humor. "Chance and Cole each have their own home. I'm the only one who sleeps in here, and I usually sleep in the middle."

"Great." She grabbed one of the extra pillows and tucked it between them. It helped a little. Turning her back to him, she plumped the pillow under her head and tried to get comfortable. It was chilly in the room; the temperature really dropped here at night. She reached down toward her feet and grabbed the extra cover. Spreading it over her, she once again plumped her pillow and tried to find a comfortable position.

Silence filled the room. Victoria closed her eyes. It felt really odd to be sharing a bed with her husband with a pillow crammed in between them.

"Wade?" she whispered. "Are you asleep?"

"No."

"It feels funny."

"What feels funny?"

"Sleeping in the same bed with my husband and having a pillow stuffed between us."

"I didn't put it there," he muttered. With a brief movement, he pulled it from between them and sent it flying across the room. "Problem solved."

"I was trying not to smush you."

"Sweetheart, you couldn't *smush* me if you tried. Don't worry about the bed. If you end up on top of me by the morning, there will be no complaints from this side."

"I know this should feel normal, but—"

Wade rolled onto his other side to face her. He propped himself up by the elbow and leaned in toward her ear. "One night is all it will take to feel normal."

Victoria was quiet. One night of what? One night of sleeping in the same bed? One night of feeling his warmth next to her? One night of making love?

Any of the three would work.

"You're right." Whatever he meant.

"Roll over, away from me," he said in a deep, rich voice. She did as asked, and his arm came around her, just below her breasts. "Okay?"

"Yes."

"Good. If you get too hot during the night, be sure to wake me up." He kissed her on the neck. "Mmm. You smell good."

She lay with her head on the pillow and Wade's arm around her. Her back was warmed by his tight abs and powerful chest. She could feel his erection against her bottom and fought not to shift against it. She could hear her heart beating in her ears and struggled to breathe normally.

She couldn't say how long she lay in that position, but it grew hot. Who was she kidding? Wade was a man in every sense of the word, and he knew how to please a woman. She knew it in every cell in her body. And he knew exactly what he was doing to her.

"Wade, are you asleep?"

"What's wrong, sweetheart?" he asked in an innocent voice.

"It's hot."

She heard him chuckle before he turned her over to face him. His lips covered hers, and his hands got busy making it a lot hotter.

After a quick shower, she dressed in jeans, a cool blouse and her new sneakers, then hurried down the stairs.

"Ready to do a little exploring?"

"Absolutely."

Victoria glanced around as she stepped off the bottom stair. Wade was standing next to the kitchen bar, a shirt held in one hand, a letter in the other. Whatever its contents, it had captured his attention and the way he was dressed captured hers. He was wearing jeans— tight, worn, ripped jeans that hugged his body like a second skin. Above the leather belt, a tight six-pack led upward to a broad chest and wide shoulders. The muscles underneath his skin moved like well-oiled steel cables. She'd never seen him dressed in anything but a suit or jogging pants. But in jeans, he was…amazing. It didn't take a pair of tight jeans for her to know that, but they served as a great reminder.

"The sugar and cream are on the table. Do you want something to eat?"

He reached out for his cup of coffee, taking a sip, then setting it on the bar without taking his eyes off the letter. Did the man not know the effect he had on women? On this woman, at least? It was like some-one put all the world's sexier-than-hell ingredients in a pan and stirred. The final product stood nonchalantly in front of her. And his innocent manner just made it worse. Or better, as it were.

When she didn't answer the question, he looked up. "Victoria?"

"What? Oh. Uh. No. Not hungry." She turned away as she felt the blush spread over her face.

"You don't look like you had a good night."

"I had a very good night." She smiled at him. "I re-quire very little sleep."

"Good thing," he said and winked.

"Do you have something I can take along to drink on the trail? Maybe a lemonade?"

She realized she was staring at him again. She couldn't help it. He frowned, no doubt sensing some-thing was up. She turned toward the fridge and her hand accidently brushed against some glasses on the counter. Scrambling, she managed to catch them before they fell and shattered. He tilted his head and those golden-brown eyes glittered wickedly as though he'd just realized the effect he was having on her.

"You up for a horseback ride?"

"Uh, yeah. Sure."

"Have you ever ridden horses before?"

Victoria just shrugged.

"Right. Well, we're going to find out. Did you find a lemonade?"

"A what?"

"You were looking for a lemonade…"

"Oh, right. I found a Diet Coke. That will do."

"Then let's go." He swung his shirt around his shoulders and pushed his muscled arms into the long sleeves. Then he proceeded to fasten the front, button by button. For Victoria, it was torture.

They returned to the massive barn, where two horses stood saddled and ready. Wade pointed to the Tobiano paint she'd loved when she'd seen it the day before. Following instinct, she took the reins and approached the mare from the animal's left side. Using the portable steps made it easy to reach the stirrups, and soon she was in the saddle and ready to go. She shot a grin of accomplishment at Wade, who nodded his head with approval. He mounted a nice chestnut gelding and they were off.

It didn't take very long to get the feel of the paint mare. The Tennessee Walker was well trained and had a smooth gait. After an hour Victoria felt as though she'd been riding all her life.

They followed the river that snaked through the Masterses' property for miles, through stands of pine and over occasional hills with views that were picture-book quality. Wade seemed completely at home in the saddle. Even to someone who was not used to horses, it was clear he'd been riding pretty much his entire life. This ranch was his home. The wind that blew through the trees called to him. The crisp morning air fed his spirit. Here, he was in his element. Victoria liked who she was with now.

"Are you getting hungry?" Wade asked from beside her. "It's almost one o'clock."

"I could eat." She nodded. "But I don't think we'll find a restaurant out here."

"You might be surprised." He grinned.

Sure enough, the trail they'd been following took a sharp curve to the right and went steadily uphill, away from the river. When they reached the top, Victoria immediately spotted a quilt spread out over the grass and a picnic basket placed in the center. It was an area that bordered a steep cliff, and a view of the whole valley was before her.

Quickly dismounting, she tied the mare by her halter rope to a nearby tree and hurried to the blanket. "Oh, my gosh, Wade! The view is breathtaking."

Wade dismounted and joined her. "This was one of my favorite places to come as a kid. Just over this hill—" he nodded to his right "—the river catches up with it, and there are some good places to fish."

She looked at him and smiled.

"So how are you doing with the horse?" he asked.

"Good, I think. She is amazing. So easy to ride." Victoria looked out over the terrain. "I just can't believe the beauty of this place. You need to have a painting done and hang it in your house."

"My mother was the artist of the family. She did landscapes, portraits. You'll see the paintings displayed in most of the buildings on the property. I don't know if she ever got up here. I don't remember seeing one depicting this view."

"That's a shame."

"Do you paint, Victoria?"

"I don't know. I must have done some before the accident, because right now I'm itching to have a charcoal pencil and a sketch pad. But whether it's just being caught in the moment of this beautiful place or if I really can paint, I couldn't tell you."

"We should go into town and get you some paints and a couple of canvases."

She shook her head. "That's too much trouble. But some paper and pencils would be great." The idea of getting some of the beautiful places she'd seen this morning on canvas intrigued her, but better to take small steps. Her phone had been destroyed in the accident. Pictures would have been great.

After they had finished their meal and a shared bottle of wine on the bluff overlooking the valley, they mounted their horses and continued down the trail, again finding the river. Through tree-covered hillsides and grassy pastures flanking the river, they made their way farther north.

"Oh, Wade. Look. It's an old house." To her right, set back in the trees, was a very old cabin made of logs complete with a chimney rising over the wooden roof.

"It's an old trappers' cabin," Wade said. "Men would set up camp here while they hunted for fresh game in the hills. We've got a couple of those dotting the property here and there."

"I want to see," Victoria said as she scrambled off her horse.

The old door was barely on its hinges, but she pushed it open enough to see inside. It had a dirt floor and two small bed frames, along with a crumbling rock fireplace. It was rustic, to say the least.

"How old do you think this is?" she asked Wade.

"Don't really know. It was probably built before my grandfather bought the land, so that would make it about a hundred and fifty years old." He dismounted. "When we were kids, we used to roam all over this area. Take enough supplies to last us three or four days. One time we came upon an old homestead. There was a cottage and what was left of a picket fence, and a barn next to it. We found an old high-top shoe and a silver comb inside the house. I think Holly still has them. If you're a history buff, you've come to the right place."

Wade walked over to her and put his arm around her shoulders. She turned to face him, and he covered her lips with his own for a kiss that was entirely too brief. "I could go on doing this forever," he said. "But we'd better head back if we want to arrive before dark."

"Okay," she agreed, standing on her tiptoes to give him another kiss. "I wish I had a phone. I would love to have a picture of this cabin."

"We will have to get you a new one. Until then, you're welcome to use mine," he said as he handed her his cell. "No reason we can't come back again."

She happily snapped off a few photos before returning his phone. Wade handed her the reins of her horse. "There's ninety-two thousand acres to roam through. Next time, we might go a different direction and find something even more to your liking."

Victoria grinned. She didn't know if she'd ever been horseback riding in her life. But it would definitely be a part of her future.

Ten

The next morning Wade climbed the steps to the back door of Pine House cabin. He saw Victoria through the window, sitting at the kitchen bar sipping a cup of coffee.

"Morning," he said as he stepped in the door.

"Good morning," she replied as he placed a large sack and its contents on the table.

"This is yours," he said, watching her.

"For me?"

In the bag was a sketch pad, drawing pencils, a small set of oil paints and two canvases. There were also brushes and a small easel that could be set up on a tabletop.

"Oh, my gosh. I hope you didn't waste your time and money."

"We'll find out," he grinned.

"Thank you, Wade." She ran into his arms and gave him a tight squeeze.

She grabbed the sketch pad and selected a pencil and soon was hard at the task of drawing the little cabin they'd seen yesterday. He left her to take care of some business calls.

Early in the afternoon, Wade returned to the kitchen. As soon as he walked into the room, his eyes grew wide in amazement. Sketches, beautiful sketches, covered every available surface. There were several of the old cabin, the river valley, one of a mother cow grazing while her baby enjoyed its lunch. There were close-ups of pinecones hanging from the branches of a tree, all detailed, all remarkable. Some were taped to the cabinet doors, others covered the countertop, even the stovetop and chairs. Victoria was at the kitchen table hard at work on yet another one. The detail in the drawings was amazing.

"Victoria?"

His voice seemed to bring her out of whatever trance she was in.

"Hi." She gave him a grin.

He walked over, kissed her, then picked up a sheet of the sketch paper, frowning as he looked closely at the drawing. "How long have you been an artist?"

She sat back and looked around her. "I didn't know I could draw." She shrugged.

"I'm assuming it just felt right," he said, using her own words. "We don't have to go anywhere today. If you like, why don't you try out the paints and do the old cabin on canvas?"

"I would love to. Are you sure you wouldn't mind?"

"Not a bit."

Wade was stunned by the artistry that had flowed from her hands. How had he never picked up on the fact that Victoria was an accomplished artist? This was no small thing. The drawings were professional and brilliant. He wanted to ask where she'd studied but knew she wouldn't remember. While their time together had always been limited, how could he never have picked up on her amazing talent?

She didn't waste any time opening the small box of colors and setting the canvas on the easel. She chose from among a dozen brushes of various sizes and shapes and got to work.

"I'm going to head over to the loafing shed and take a look at some new heifers. I'll be back in about an hour and we'll have lunch."

"Okay," she responded, already pressing some colors onto the palette. By the time he stepped outside, Victoria was already absorbed in what she was doing.

Early that evening, Wade stood just inside the back door, looking over her shoulder at the painting in progress. He whistled, low and long. "That is spectacular, Victoria. I never knew you had such talent."

"Thank you. I can't say if it's good or not, but it feels good to have a brush in my hand. Are you ready for lunch?" she asked, wiping her hands on a dish towel she'd found beneath one of the cabinets.

"Lunch has come and gone, darling. It's after seven. I came back around three, and you were really into your painting, so I just left you alone. I came back to see if you wanted dinner. You really should eat something. A starving artist isn't necessarily a good thing."

"Okay. You're right. Let me clean up my mess and we can go."

It was a short walk to where the ranch hands congregated every night around the campfire. Tonight chili was the main course. As before, Victoria got her serving and sat next to Wade on the tree stump. Tonight there were guitars, and soon music filled the air around them. It was a cool evening with a light breeze out of the south. Victoria seemed contented watching fireflies light the night. There was a full moon overhead.

"I'm so glad you brought me here. I have a feeling I haven't felt this relaxed in a very long time. I hope… I hope it's not the last time we come here."

"We'll come back, sweetheart. I promise. But we need to get back to Dallas. There is a meeting that Cole and I both need to attend next week concerning a merger we've both been involved in. I was notified this morning that the other parties are ready to sit down and hash this thing out. Apparently things have progressed since I was last in Japan."

"That's always the excuse," a man chimed in behind them.

Wade immediately grinned and stood up as the man

came into view. He was as tall as Wade and had the same muscular physique, the same stance.

"How're you doing, bro? How was the flight in?"

"Good. I wanted to say hello and meet your bride. Holly told me you finally brought Victoria to the ranch."

"Victoria." Wade looked down to where she sat. "This is my younger brother, Chance. You met his wife, Holly, the day we arrived. Chance, this is Victoria."

She immediately rose. "It's very nice to meet you."

"And you as well." Chance shook her hand. "Wade treating you right?"

"So far. Can't complain."

"Ha! Give it time," Chance teased. "I'm glad you brought her out to the ranch. We all thought you'd made her up."

"Nope, she's as real as they come."

"Welcome to the family, Victoria. Glad to have you with us."

"Thank you."

Wade accompanied Chance as he made the rounds, saying hello to the ranch hands around the fire. The brothers had that certain something that made them stand out in a crowd. Both were strong, powerful men in their own right.

"I talked with Cole just a few minutes ago," Chance told Wade. "They are on a flight back from London. He said you were here and asked me to remind you that you both have an appointment with a Mr. Taka-hashi on Monday."

"I know," Wade replied. "We're going to have to

get back to Dallas tomorrow. How did the meeting in London go?"

"Very well, according to Cole. Synecom will soon be a part of Masters International. They will merge with the pharmaceutical division by the end of the year. Loudon Deeming, the president and CEO, is reportedly excited to have his company involved with ours."

"Excellent."

"Oh," Chance added. "One other thing. Cole said the date for the probate of Dad's will has been set. Seth is expected to fly down. I'm glad he'll be here."

"Me, too," Wade agreed. "He's a good man. Seth is our half brother," he explained to Victoria. "He lives in California."

"Well, take care you two. Have a good trip home." Chance looked at Victoria. "Again, it was really nice to meet you."

"You as well."

Bidding the ranch hands a good night, Chance disappeared into the darkness as he headed to his truck. No doubt Holly was awaiting his return.

Wade hated like hell to leave Victoria alone when he had to conduct business, especially since she still didn't have her memory back. But at least now, with her art, she would have plenty to keep her occupied. That thought had run through his mind more than once today. And maybe it would even be therapeutic and help her heal. For the first time, Wade really hoped things could work out between them.

When they got back to Dallas, he was going to find

a specialist, someone trained in memory recall. Surely there was some way to give her back her full life. It was only then that they would be able to have a full life together. After the time he'd spent in her company since the accident, he couldn't believe he'd ever thought she could be hateful or deceitful. He didn't have an answer as to why she had changed over the days since the accident. But he was not willing to let her go back to the way she was. Whatever he had to do to accomplish that end, he would do it.

"Are you about ready to go?" Wade asked, holding his hand out to her.

"Sure," she replied and stood up, taking his hand.

They tossed their paper bowls and plastic silverware into the trash and headed to the log home on the hill. He put his arm around her shoulders, her arm went around his back and together they walked toward Pine House.

After a second day of horseback riding, they cooled off from the afternoon sun near a small waterfall. It was nothing like the one at his home in Dallas, but it had a beauty all its own. At the bottom of the falls was a natural pool, again about half the size of his pool in Dallas. But this one was created by the elements eons ago. They swam and splashed and laughed, then dried off on one of the big boulders adjacent to the pool.

"How about we head back and give you time to pack for our trip home and get ready for tonight?" Wade asked. "Our reservations are at seven. That means we should leave here by five or five thirty if we go in the chopper. I would highly recommend that means of travel. It's beautiful at night."

"Reservations?"

"Yeah. When we get back to Dallas, I thought we would stop and eat at a restaurant I know. Really great food. After we eat, I thought you might enjoy going to an art exhibit on our way home."

"I'd love to!" She sat up, leaned over and kissed him. "You're too good to me," she whispered against his lips. "I don't deserve you."

"Woman, you've got that reversed."

His lips covered hers as he rolled her over to show her just how glad he was to share this moment with her. But by later in the day, he'd grown impatient. Twenty minutes after five, he stood at the bottom of the staircase, waiting. But fifteen minutes later when Victoria finally did come down the stairs, the slight frustration of having to wait disappeared in a puff of smoke. She had changed into a black dress that softly glimmered as she walked, hugging her every curve. It came down to about six inches above her knees.

It was draped low in the back, making a perfect frame for her hair, which was pulled back, letting soft curls cascade from the crown of her head. She had added makeup, but it was so subtle it served only to enhance her delicate features. As if they needed enhancing. Her lips were a deep, sultry red. Quite honestly, he had never seen her so beautiful. He swallowed hard.

"You look ravishing," he said in greeting. The dress, along with the combination of the heady scent of perfume and Victoria's own erotic aroma, nearly brought him to his knees. "Where... How did you get the dress?"

"Every girl always needs that little black dress just in case."

He kissed her neck, cupping her face and trying hard not to scoop her off her feet and carry her to the closest bedroom. Or the kitchen table. Or the sofa in the den.

"I want to take you right now," he said against her lips before deepening the kiss. "I haven't a clue how I'm ever going to get through this evening."

She laughed. "We'd better go. That's a subject for later."

"And it will be addressed. Or undressed as the case may be."

They ate at a restaurant located some fifty stories up. The glass-dome enclosure slowly revolved, giving them a panoramic view of the lights of downtown Dallas.

Dinner was delicious. Wade watched Victoria with a glint in his eyes. She guessed he was thinking about the end of the evening when they returned home. And a little bird told her it was going to be quite a night. He was so male, so strong, so handsome. Behind closed doors he knew how to make love like no other. She looked forward to getting home.

Dinner finished, they took the glass elevator down to street level and entered a waiting limo to head to the art exhibit. Victoria was thrilled at the prospect of seeing a gallery show for the first time since her accident. Wade picked up on her nervous energy and folded his large hand over hers. She smiled at him through the darkness, so grateful that he would take the time to do this for her.

When they got to the gallery, Wade confirmed his reservations for the evening with an attendant in the front lobby. "Good evening, Mr. Masters," the woman said. "It's so nice to have you both with us this evening. Take your time and enjoy. I'll be here if you have any questions."

"This isn't a public showing?" Victoria asked once they were out of hearing distance. She noticed that the people in attendance were exquisitely dressed.

"Nah. We're doing this privately. You couldn't enjoy it nearly as much with people crowding around the paintings. Have a glass of champagne." He took one for each of them from the tray of a passing waiter. "Go at your own speed, and look to your heart's content. A friend of mine owns the gallery. These are paintings from various artists that have been sold but have yet to be shipped."

Most of the paintings near the front were abstract. On the wall underneath each canvas was a typed label with the name of the piece, the date it was created and sometimes but not always the name of the artist who painted it. Victoria stood there, fascinated by the brushstrokes and colors. They slowly walked through the space, and the paintings became less abstract. There were pictures of bridges, geese flying over a tranquil lake, clouds over a green field with the rain imminent. It all stirred something deep within Victoria.

As she turned to leave, one painting in particular caught her eye. It was a snapshot view of a farm with a small white house. A storm was coming, the sky already dark. The lady of the house was outside with her clothes basket, trying to bring in the wash from the line, with sheets blowing in every direction and bolts of lightning in the not-too-distant background. Victoria stepped over to the painting. Again there was no artist name, just the year it was painted and the title of the painting: *Storm Is Coming*. She couldn't stop her hand from reaching out to the painting, but she stopped short of touching it as she continued studying the detail. A shiver ran up her spine. She'd seen it before. She was sure of it.

"You like that one?" Wade asked from behind her.

She turned to face him. "Wade, I know this painting. I mean, I've seen it before."

"Maybe the fact you remember it means your memory is coming back."

"Oh, I hope so."

He nodded. "The artist's style reminds me of yours."

She looked even more closely but only found initials in the lower right-hand corner of the canvas: *L.D.*

"Can we find out who the artist is?" she asked Wade.

"Let me make an inquiry. I'll be right back."

Victoria wandered on through the gallery, taking in the statues and other creations of art. By the time Wade returned, Victoria was in heaven yet a bit unsettled by the whole experience. All this beauty had her in its grip. The amount of talent represented here was overwhelming. And the style of the paintings was somehow familiar.

"The painting you asked about is by a relatively new artist. Laurel Dawson. She lives outside the Dallas metroplex to the south. This painting has been sold, but they have our name should she return with any more paintings."

She couldn't thank Wade enough.

Once back at the helipad, they quickly boarded the chopper and began the ride home. The helicopter took a slow path around Dallas. Wade had been right. The lights were amazing. He leaned over and took her in his arms.

All in all, it had been a remarkable evening. A fairytale night. But even in the arms of the man she loved, sailing through the darkness in a flying chariot, she still carried that tiny feeling of trepidation that all was not right. Wade picked up on it.

"What's the matter, Victoria?"

"Nothing." She shrugged and touched his cheek. "This trip has all been so great. I think I'm just sad that it's over. I already miss the ranch."

"We'll go back again. The Governor's Ball is coming up next month. It's an event you usually look forward to. I had completely forgotten about it, but my assistant just sent a reminder. This is a charity we sponsor each year. You need to have your dress fittings, and I've got some work I must see to before then. But I had your art supplies sent ahead to the house. You should have plenty to keep you busy."

"The Governor's Ball?" she asked. "Wade, I can't go to something like that."

"Why not?" He frowned.

"I won't know anyone. I won't remember anything, what to do, how to react… I can't go to something so important. I haven't even been out of the house to speak of."

"Victoria, it's just an annual event for charity. The people there won't know if you remember them or not. It just isn't a big deal."

"It sounds like a very big deal."

"The designer will come to refit your dress. And we will attend together. Don't worry."

"I would imagine there's quite a bit of work waiting for you, especially knowing how much time I caused you to miss."

Wade lowered the mic and kissed her on the end of her nose. "I haven't had any time off since… I can't remember. The company is at a point where it pretty much runs itself day-to-day. I have to step in for mergers and certain other corporate dealings, but Cole is there to handle things almost every day. Once he gets back from London and we take care of a few matters, including our conference call Monday morning, I should have more time to spend with you."

"It must be a big deal if you're both needed on the call."

"When you're dealing with foreign dignitaries, it helps to have backup." He lowered her mouthpiece for the mic and leaned over and stole a kiss. He held her eyes with his as he replaced both microphones. "It won't take long, I promise. I should be back by late afternoon."

"Take as long as you need. Your business comes first. I'll sleep in, paint and enjoy the pool while you're gone."

"Be careful of the pool—" he began, and Victoria cut him off.

"I will, and we've had this discussion."

"I'll agree to you sleeping in, getting some rest." He raised his microphone and pulled her headset away from her ear. "'Cause you're gonna need it," he said against her ear, his voice low and sexy. He replaced the microphone and sat back satisfied as a fat pampered cat.

The chopper landed on the Masterses' private airfield, and the pilot killed the motor. A car was waiting to take them to the mansion. The sounds in the city were so different from the ranch. There, while they'd eaten their dinner, in the distance the coyotes howled at the moon, cows mooed and birds sang their song.

It was a short ride from the landing pad to the mansion. Once they reached the house, Victoria excused herself to take a quick shower and change her clothes. When she stepped under the gentle spray in the shower enclosure, she regulated the heat and shampooed her hair. With her eyes closed, she didn't see Wade step into the shower. His big hands, loaded with soap, proceeded to lather every inch of her body. Her heartbeat tripled at knowing he was here with her. He paid special attention to her breasts, which swelled under his touch. Then his hands moved lower, gently rubbing the sensitive area between her legs. He knelt before her, his mouth finding and enjoying the little nub of her womanhood.

Just as Victoria lost the strength to stand, he stood and grabbed her hips, lifting her to him. Her back was against the cool wall of the shower, the water coming down all around her. She gasped as Wade settled her onto his erection. With one push, he was all the way inside her. Her legs came around his hips, her arms around his neck as he began to move.

"I can't hold it back for long, Victoria. I have no willpower where you're concerned."

She could only nod her head in understanding.

He began to move faster and faster, pumping into her until they both were frantic for release. Wade pulled out, picked her up and carried her to the bedroom, drying her with a soft blanket before helping her onto the bed. He reached into the nightstand drawer for a silver packet and quickly got it open and slipped the condom into place. Then he was inside her again, working his magic and bringing them both to the edge of ecstasy. Victoria let out a cry and felt the electric current run down her spine as her body detonated. She held on to Wade with all the strength she had left. Wade followed seconds later. She glowed in the aftermath, listening to his heart beating in a rhythm as fast as her own, surrounded by the warmth and the scent of this man she loved.

After holding her and allowing time for them both to catch their breath, he reached over to the night table and picked up a small black velvet case. He held it out to her. Victoria sat up, not fully understanding. When he opened the lid, there was the most exquisite diamond ring in the world. Wade took it out of the box and took her left hand.

"I realized, belatedly, my wife isn't wearing her wedding ring. Could it be because the other was given as merely a token to wear out in public and not with the feelings that are supposed to come with it?"

"I took it off after you told me about our marriage. It's in the drawer in the side table."

He shook his head as though it amazed him. "Will you please accept this until you can pick out your own wedding band to go with it?" he asked as he slipped it on her finger.

It was beyond breathtaking, with an enormous diamond surrounded by clusters of smaller ones. It fit perfectly. "Wade. You didn't have to do this. Especially since…well, since we are kind of only just married on paper."

"Then marry me for real, Victoria." His voice was deep and soft; his eyes indicated his sincerity. "Be mine in every way a man and a woman can be joined."

There were no words. She scrambled up on her knees to get closer, fell against him and found his lips with hers. "I love you, Wade Masters."

The next few days were the paradigm of perfection, with Victoria alternately painting and enjoying the pool while Wade went to his office. The nights were pure magic. They talked about anything and everything.

Wade told her some of what he contended with at his business, talked about his family and his childhood. Victoria hung on each and every word and hoped someday she could regain her memory and share herself with Wade in the same way.

Today, they were having lunch together at the house. It was one of the rare occasions that Wade could get away from work to be here with her during the day. They sat in the nook Victoria had designed for them, eating sandwiches and discussing her latest canvas.

"Mr. Masters," Curtis interrupted, approaching them with a tentative air. "Excuse me, sir, but your assistant is on line four."

"Excuse me, Victoria. I'd better take this."

"No, you go ahead. She probably misses you, since you're so seldom away from the office."

Wade stood from the table, kissed her on the head and disappeared. After only a few minutes, he was back.

"Everything okay?"

He nodded, sitting back down and taking up his fork and knife.

"My assistant was just updating me on the second conference call with the Japanese dignitaries next week. She has all the requested information gathered and in order. She wanted to know if there was anything else I would need."

Victoria nodded her head in understanding.

"I know," Wade said, setting his cutlery on the table and reaching for her hand. "Reality always finds a way of rearing its ugly head just about the time I start to relax and enjoy myself. It's just one of the drawbacks of being CEO of Masters International. At least I won't be coming home to an empty house. I thank you for that, Victoria."

"I love you, Wade."

"All right, that's it—I quit. I'll have my notice on… somebody's desk this afternoon."

She giggled. "I don't think you can do that. Think of all the people that are counting on you. You can't let them down."

"Seriously, thank you for understanding."

Victoria smiled. "So, what does Cinderella do at the Governor's Ball?"

"Stand in a receiving line that goes on for miles, pretend you're having a wonderful time, ensure the governor and his wife are having a wonderful time. Enjoy the desserts and dance with your husband until your feet scream *no more!* And as soon as we can get an opening, we're out of there."

Victoria laughed.

"Actually, you attended last year and didn't stop talking about it for weeks. Before the accident, you were looking forward to it this year, too, as I recall. Most of the people you encounter there are nice enough, and the music is provided by a special touring section of the Dallas Symphony Orchestra.

"But the main thing will be for you to have an enjoyable evening, make some new friends, say hello to the old ones you can't remember and know that I'll be right there with you."

"It's scary meeting the outside world without knowing anyone. It's one thing to not have my close friends—if I have any—drop by. But this…this is a big deal. It's important to you. What if I mess up?"

"You won't mess up, Victoria. The attendees will be glad to see you after news of your accident. Just try to relax and have a good time."

"Okay, then. If you're sure you're okay with what might happen, I'll do my best and let my Prince Charming escort me to the ball."

Eleven

In the days that followed, she saw less and less of Wade. But as insane as her schedule became as she prepared for the ball, she could only imagine what his must be like. At least it would only be for a few more days. Then they could return to the ranch for a while.

The dress designer and his staff had arrived for the final fitting of her gown and set up in one of the guest bedrooms. When they removed the protective cover, Victoria gasped in amazement. It was the most beautiful thing she'd ever seen. The black-sequined silk clung to her body, falling all the way to the floor, a plunging neckline and scooped back adding to the dramatic effect. Though she couldn't remember, it was more than likely the most daring dress she'd ever worn.

"Oh, madam, you have lost weight over the past few months since your original fitting," said the designer. "Still, we have time. We will take it in, and it will be perfect and ready for you before the ball."

Something about the fitting brought it all home. She was going to attend one of the most important functions in Wade's year. She wouldn't be able to remember names or faces. She would be a laughingstock and bring embarrassment to the entire family.

When Wade arrived home that evening, he immediately sensed something was wrong and asked what was the matter.

She sat in a chair staring out the bedroom window. "Nothing. I'm glad you're home."

"Honey." He tossed his jacket on the nearest chair. "Don't be concerned about the gala. It's really not a big deal. There will be over three hundred people in attendance, but you'll be the most exquisite woman there. Just stick close to my side. No one will notice if you remember them from a year ago. In fact, most of the attendees won't know I'm married, so there will be plenty of congratulations. If asked, just say we decided against a big wedding."

She nodded. What else could she do?

The next morning a package was delivered from a local art gallery. Victoria fretted for a while as to whether to open it or wait for Wade. In the end she gave in to her curiosity and pulled the brown paper away from the gold-edged frame. It was a simple painting of a Siamese cat perched on the edge of a small table,

completely absorbed in watching the antics of a butterfly in metallic blues and golds, with one paw raised in
alert concentration and fascination. The combination
of mute tones and shadows and the bright effervescent
colors of the eyes of the cat and the butterfly combined
to make a painting of near photographic quality.

She leaned in closer and gazed at the delicate brushstrokes. Despite the overall beauty of the painting, Victoria saw flaws. The fur of the cat could have been made
to appear thicker, fluffier. The eyes were the color typical of that breed of cat, but they also should have reflected the color of the objects surrounding it.

Suddenly Victoria realized she was viewing the canvas with a professional eye for detail. Her hand closed
as though she was holding a paintbrush, ready to fin-
ish an incomplete work of art, to add the tiny minute
strokes and bring the painting to its full completion.

Wade's heavy hands came to rest on her shoulders,
breaking her out of the spell. "I like it," he said, leaning over to kiss the side of her face.

"It's not finished." She frowned.

"What? Victoria, you bought this painting a few days
before the accident. You called and told me about a
small gallery you'd discovered and an up-and-coming
artist you'd met there. You said you had arranged to
have the painting delivered when the show was taken
down, which is now."

"That must be why it looks recognizable." She
shrugged, a slight headache taking hold. "I couldn't
understand where I might have seen it before, yet it

looked incredibly familiar. Maybe it's a sign of my memory returning."

"Maybe it is. We'll have it hung in the library. Seems fitting for that room. It's a beautiful painting," he added.

"I guess so." Again she leaned forward intently, gazing at the details. "But it needs to be finished before it's hung."

Wade shrugged and looked at his wife. "It looks finished to me. Are you hungry? Victoria?"

"I guess."

"Maybe your memory is returning. Familiar is a good thing."

She nodded her head.

"Come on, sweetheart," he prompted, taking her hand. "I'm starved. Don't worry about the painting. Apparently you selected it before the accident. It will all come back eventually."

She sighed, nodding. "I hope you're right."

It was now just two days until the Governor's Ball. Her gown hung in what used to be her bedroom, and her shoes had been placed on the floor beneath it. The makeup artist was scheduled to arrive four hours before they were due to leave, just after the hairdresser and manicurist finished their jobs. Everything was all set.

But Victoria's nerves were tied in knots. Wade had continually assured her it wasn't a big deal, but Victoria knew better. It was the event of the year, with a list of attending dignitaries as long as her arm. She wouldn't know anyone there. Even those she'd met last year she wouldn't recognize. That had to be the reason for her trepidation.

Wade's brothers and their wives would be in attendance. Holly had been calling every day to try to alleviate Victoria's fears, assuring her no one would notice if she forgot a name or two. Or three. Victoria wasn't convinced. But Wade was depending on her to go with him, and there was no way she would let him down.

Wade was due back from his office in a few hours, and Victoria wanted to do something nice for him. She ventured down to the kitchen area and asked the chef to prepare Wade's favorite meal to be served around seven. Every moment they had together became more and more special. She was truly in love with her husband. Head over heels.

Despite his massive wealth, she still liked him best when he was on the ranch, dressed in his worn, tight-fitting jeans, with a laid-back look on his face that said all was right with the world. And the ranch was so beautiful. She was so grateful he'd shared that part of his life.

The candles were lit and burning in the center of the small table. Jacob had brought his amazing insight to bear, apparently guessing this was to be a special night. He'd covered the table with linens and arranged a small bouquet of flowers.

She'd dressed in a daring black creation with a mesh fabric between the areas of lace that covered only the briefest parts of her anatomy. Its plunging neckline and low back finished the overall effect. Her hair was pulled back with a silver comb.

Wade arrived home a little before six thirty. His eyes lit up the instant he saw her. Then he frowned, a question forming in his eyes.

"Did I miss an invitation? Are we having guests?"

"Nope. Just the two of us."

"Mmm. Brings all sorts of possibilities to mind. You look delicious, by the way."

"Thank you," she replied. "So do you."

He grinned. That gorgeous, sexy grin that made her want to make love to him where they stood. Wade loosened his tie and shed his jacket, tossing it over a chair. "Hope you don't mind. I'm going to take a shower." He leaned over and kissed her.

Smiling, Victoria followed him up the stairs. "The sea bass will be ready in about half an hour."

"That may be too soon."

"Too soon?"

He entered his suite and walked to the phone, dialing the kitchen. "Yeah, Jacob? Put a hold on that dinner until you hear from me." He looked over at Victoria. "At least an hour. Maybe two," he said into the receiver. Hanging up, he unbuttoned his silk shirt. Next went the belt, socks and shoes. She couldn't help but notice a slight, almost devious smile cross his face.

Without preamble he approached her, spun her around and unzipped her dress. He gave it a slight push and it fell off her shoulders and onto the floor. Soon she stood before him in only her lacy bikini underwear and black heels.

"Wade, I don't understand…"

With one hand he removed the silver comb that was holding her hair back, letting it fall around her shoulders. When she turned back to him, she shook her head and her hair fanned out, just covering her breasts.

"There is only one thing I'm starving for tonight."

"And what would that be?"

"You." He dropped his pants, took off his shirt and led her to the bathroom. "Can I interest you in joining me?"

Victoria grinned. "Maybe."

"Maybe? Maybe *yes*?"

"Yes."

His lips met hers, and the kiss was deep and hungry. She could never get enough of the taste of him, of how his lips were so soft yet firm. He had his nightly stubble, which made him even sexier.

Suddenly she was in his arms, and they were standing under the shower. Without breaking their kiss, his tongue going deeper into her mouth, Wade reached down to her hip and slowly slid the silken panties down her legs.

Stepping out of her shoes, she grabbed the scented soap, worked it into suds and began washing his broad chest, down over the six-pack abs and lower to his erection. This time it was Wade's turn as she knelt before him. After rinsing off the soap, she slid her lips over his engorged penis, clutching its length with her hand.

"Victoria," he moaned.

"I want to touch you," she said, backing away momentarily. "Tell me how to do it better."

His hands cupped the back of her head, gently guiding her back to his length. "You're doing just fine." He inhaled a ragged breath. "Oh, God, Victoria!"

For a few minutes she enjoyed the feel and taste of him. Her hand slid up and down the velvety skin of his shaft while her mouth and tongue licked and teased the sensitive tip.

"Victoria, that's enough," he said in a rough voice. He lifted her to her feet. "If you continue, this will be over far too soon."

He turned her around and, after lathering her hair, proceeded to wash her breasts, then run his hands down over her waist and belly. He palmed her mound before spreading her folds, making her weak with joy. She lost all the strength in her legs yet, needing more of what he was giving, managed to stay on her feet. He reached out and gripped her arms to steady her, then turned her toward him. Grasping her hips, he lifted her up and onto his erection. Pausing to line up with her core, he pushed inside. Her head lay back against the shower wall, so engaged in what he was doing she couldn't think of anything but Wade. He placed his open palm against her neck, his thumb under her jaw, and he began to move. His movements became faster and faster until, with a cry, Victoria fell apart and Wade followed, calling out her name.

She had a few seconds to catch her breath before he covered her with a warmed towel, scooped her up and carried her into the bedroom. After drying them both, he threw back the covers and laid her down.

He opened his lips to hers, and her arms went around his neck. He moved from her lips to her neck, taking small nips and bestowing kisses down to her breasts. Where Wade touched, her body came alive. With his hands he kneaded the firm skin of her breasts, taking the swollen tips into his mouth, sucking hard, first one, then the other.

Victoria arched her back in response.

"Wade," she whimpered.

"What, sweetheart?" he said. "Tell me what you need, Victoria."

As an answer, she reached down and found his swollen shaft. The tip had a droplet of moisture, and she took pleasure in rubbing it over his erection before guiding him toward her opening.

He smiled in the darkness. "Not yet, sweetheart." He began to kiss his way farther down the feminine curves of her body.

Taking his time, he continued to trail kisses down over her stomach and on to that special place between her legs. Pushing her legs wide apart, he dived in, tasting of her essence, using his tongue to drive her wild. Victoria sucked the air deep into her lungs as she was consumed with sensation. A pressure began to build within her. For a moment the world stopped turning and everything went still. Then she felt completely out of control as electric currents shot down her spine in a pulse-pounding climax. Wade stayed with her until she quieted, then pushed off the bed, quickly slid a condom into place and returned. She was exhausted, but his mouth and hands transformed fatigue into need. Soon she was ready for him again. He slid into her, filling her.

He began to move, this time taking it slow, loving her in the only way he knew how. With each stroke, the intensity grew.

"Are you up for trying something new?" he asked against her ear, his deep voice causing chills to run across her overheated skin.

"Yes," she answered breathlessly. With Wade, she'd try anything.

He pulled out and rolled her onto her stomach. Grasping her hips, he pulled her up and toward him. Holding her hips, he gently worked his swollen shaft into her from the back. She grabbed the silken sheets with her hands.

"Okay?"

She nodded. "Yes."

Slowly he began to move. Victoria couldn't hold back the moan of delight. His hand came between them, and he gently massaged the intensely sensitive nub between her folds. Wade was a master at sex, raw sex. Between his thrusts and what his hand was doing, in seconds she cried out, her inner core tightening against him in climax. That was all it took to push him over the edge. Wade ensured her climax went on and on, milking it to the very end, pushing inside her over and over again until finally he collapsed to her side.

He brushed her long hair away from her face. "Now,

what were you planning for dinner?" he asked, breathing hard.

She smiled. "I think we just had dessert."

"No, Victoria. That was only the first course."

He felt her kiss his sweaty chest and neck. The heat they had created felt like a vapor, covering them both in the warm aftermath of sex.

He couldn't believe how much she had come to mean to him. How much he wanted her memory to return so that they could have a full, rich relationship. It bothered him how heavily the amnesia weighed on her. Her apprehension about attending the ball was only one of the ways it played out.

He gently rolled her onto her side so he could spoon her to sleep, with one arm tucked under her head and the other around her side and under her breasts. His erection was already coming back to life against her bottom. She smelled of patchouli and spices from the soap and a delicious scent that was all her own.

After the gala was over and behind them, he wanted to give her a wedding, the wedding of her dreams. Let her go as big or small as she wanted. And a honeymoon; wherever on this earth she wanted to go, he would take her.

How this remarkable romance had come to pass, he didn't quite know. It was definitely against the odds that she would wake up from an accident and be someone he wanted to spend the rest of his life with. Because of her sincerity and gentle nature, her love of adventure and her ability to tug at his heart, he was quite sure he was falling in love with Victoria, and this time around it was for real.

Twelve

Victoria sleepily turned over, smiling as she heard Wade's snoring. She loved to lie awake and listen to him as he slept, to feel the warmth of his body and kiss him when he didn't know she was doing it. And she couldn't help but notice that the beautiful diamond on her left hand glittered even in the subdued lighting of the room.

She glanced at the clock; it was just past midnight. The thought of some milk and a snack suddenly stirred her appetite. Grinning, she slipped into her nightgown and robe and left their bedroom, descending the stairs. Soon she was standing in the immense kitchen. Before she could open the refrigerator, she heard a sound at the side entrance. She turned in time to see someone push open the door and step inside. As soon as she approached the doorway, she spotted a woman turned away from her, shaking out an umbrella from the light mist that was falling outside.

A twinge of fear raced down her spine. "Uh…hello? How can I help you?"

The woman slowly turned to face her.

And all the breath left Victoria's lungs as she looked into her own face.

Who was this woman and what did she want? Before Victoria could ask, she felt a searing pain in her head.

"I see you've been having quite the time in my absence," the woman said. Her eyes narrowed as she looked at Victoria from head to foot. "Just what in the hell do you think you're doing?"

"I…don't understand. I don't… Who are you?" The white walls and alabaster floor began to tilt. She felt a severe headache coming on like she hadn't experienced in months; the pounding in her temples was excruciating.

"You were supposed to be out of here by now," the woman raged, stepping still closer to Victoria. "Instead, you convince my husband to take you on a damn joyride. How nice for you. But it's over. It's done. I want you out of my house. *Now.*"

"*Your* house?" She raised a hand to her throbbing head. Visions began to whirl in her mind. Random pictures of her art studio. Of Murphy, her rescue dog. And of this woman threatening to blackmail her if she didn't play along with her scheme.

"Don't even go there, you little bitch. Why wouldn't you answer my calls?" She was screaming now, becoming more enraged by the second. "Just what in hell did you think you were going to accomplish? Oh…maybe you thought Wade would fall in love and forgive our little game plan." She snorted in disgust. "Sorry to break the news, honey, but Wade Masters will never love anything or anyone. He's a cold, calculating bastard. But that's my problem, not yours. Where is he, by the way?"

"He's…upstairs." *In the bed where we just made love.*

"Here?" she screeched. "Wade is here? You've got to get out. You must leave immediately. My car is still outside. Take it, and get out of here before he comes downstairs. I'll meet you at the studio tomorrow. *Go!*"

Victoria was in serious pain. She couldn't stop the memories from slamming into her mind. Absently, she reached for the top of the cabinet and held on as the room continued to spin.

"What's wrong with you? Didn't you understand what I just said?" The woman walked over to where Victoria stood clutching the cabinet. "Leave now. Get out!"

"What in the hell is going on?" Wade stepped into the room.

It took the woman almost a full minute to regain her composure. "Why don't you ask her," she snarled. "I've been on a short vacation, and this woman apparently decided to take my place while I was gone."

"That's not true." Her mind was whirling as the

memories came flooding back. She remembered. She remembered everything.

Laurel. Her name was Laurel. Not Victoria.

Victoria Masters had come into her art studio in Waxahachie and bought a painting. She had introduced herself as Laurel's aunt. The resemblance was uncanny.

Over a cup of coffee that day, Victoria had explained that, decades ago, her much older sister had landed on tough times and had a child in poverty and died giving birth. Victoria had recently found a small box of old pictures at her mother's house and asked who they were photos of. One in particular was of a newborn baby. Her mother had finally admitted the child was Victoria's niece. Laurel was that child. Hence the family resemblance—they were practically twins.

Laurel had been raised in a series of foster homes, so this seemed nothing short of a miracle. She didn't know she had any family let alone an aunt. Yet Victoria had tracked her down. To have a real family was more than she'd ever dreamed of. Laurel was delighted to meet Victoria. She could barely sleep that night in the hopes of seeing her again.

Victoria had come back two days later, this time saying she needed a huge favor. She needed to leave the country for a few months and offered Laurel a large sum of money to take her place during that time. To stay in her home and pretend to be Victoria. She assured her that her husband was in Europe, and no one would ever find out. With the right hairstyle and makeup, no one would question who Laurel really was.

Laurel couldn't imagine pretending to be someone else. Trying to fool anyone like that would be ridiculous, and immoral. Laurel had refused. She wouldn't know how to be another person. But Victoria would not accept her answer. She had been prepared for Laurel to decline before she walked in the door.

Victoria had pushed back, demanding Laurel do as she wanted. But Laurel again turned her down, refusing the money. That had been when Victoria turned from nice to vicious, threatening her, saying she would ruin her in the art world if she didn't agree and assured her she had the clout to do so.

Art was all Laurel had. It had been her dream most of her life. If she lost that…she hated to think what she would do or where she would go. The art community was close-knit. Especially among those commanding top prices and whose paintings were world-renowned. She knew she had what it took to make her childhood dream come true and was beginning to show here and there in galleries. And now this person threatened to ruin it all if Laurel didn't pretend to be her for three months. Victoria had thrown out several names of the more prestigious art dealers in the area, claiming to know each personally. Victoria was a very good client and they would have no trouble turning away a wannabe if she asked. Laurel had felt her dreams begin to fade. This was surreal.

Victoria had assured her she was married to a billionaire who stayed out of the country 90 percent of the time. Laurel would live in his mansion and basically do as she wanted for those three months. Shopping sprees, museums—she could even build her own temporary art studio and paint to her heart's content. "Do it," she had insisted. "What do you have to lose except your livelihood? It's three short months."

Laurel had asked, "Why? What's the reason you need me to do this? What's so important?"

Victoria had snarled at her. "It's none of your damn business. Just do as you're told. I assure you the less you know, the better."

"Is it because you're pregnant?" Laurel had quietly asked. Great pains had been taken to conceal Victoria's condition, but her efforts were not good enough. She looked to be about six or seven months along.

"That's none of your business!" she'd retorted. "Now, take this key and write down the passwords. A car is waiting to take you to the house."

"Now?"

"Right now."

Laurel had had no choice but to agree, although how she was going to manage to carry out the ridiculous scheme, she didn't know. She had worked too long and too hard, kept her dream alive through too much to take a chance that this woman could bring it all to a screeching halt. If that happened, she would have nothing.

She had called her best friend, Beth Hamilton, and told her she'd been invited to stay at a friend's house for a few months, promising she would be in touch. Victoria had arranged for a limo to pick her up and Laurel had left the studio in Victoria's chauffeur-driven Lexus, keys and pass codes in hand, when an eighteen-wheeler ran a red light and plowed into them. By the time she reached the hospital, the real Victoria was on her way to Paris.

Now Victoria was back and telling lies, blaming all of this on Laurel. Wade looked beside himself, staring at the two nearly identical women in the same room. "Will one of you tell me what in the hell is going on?"

"She's an intruder. Can't you see what has happened?" Victoria snipped. "I told you, I've been away. I returned home this evening and found this woman in *my* house."

He glared at Victoria, then at Laurel until she wanted to curl up and die.

"Wade, it isn't what it looks like," Laurel began to explain. Her head pounded as she reeled with all of the memories suddenly released in her mind. "She approached me and asked if I would pose as her while she was out of the country."

His eyes shot fire. "You agreed to that?"

Tears welled in Victoria's eyes. "Not at first. But eventually, yes," she whispered. "I did, but it wasn't like she's making it sound."

"What in the hell is your name, anyway?" he demanded.

"Laurel. Laurel Dawson."

"You're a very good actress, Laurel Dawson. I assume the amnesia was all a ruse as well?"

"No, Wade…"

"It doesn't matter now, darling. I'm back. Just let it go," Victoria stated.

Wade glared at the other woman. "Where have you been for all these months, Victoria?"

She breezed over to Wade. "I've been in Paris. Remember, I told you. We were going to meet last week at the Café Le Bruin. But you never showed up."

"Why fly all the way to Paris when I thought it was you here with me?" Obviously Wade hadn't gone to meet Victoria there, since he thought she was at home, recovering from her accident. And in his bed.

"Victoria came to my studio," Laurel began, knowing Wade was listening but doubting every word. "She said she was my aunt and wanted to take advantage of our resemblance and asked me to take her place. I refused."

"Right," Victoria interjected. "We can see how well that went. What a lie. Honestly, Wade, I don't have a clue what she's talking about. And while our appearance might be similar, I certainly don't have a niece my own age. You know Mother and Father. Do you really think that's possible?"

"You were pregnant," Laurel stated. "You went to Paris to have your baby."

That got Wade's attention. He directed his hard gaze back at Victoria, and now Victoria was seething. She began screaming and cursing, going so far as to approach Laurel with her hand raised as though to slap her. Wade intervened, and the two began a heated battle, one Laurel wanted to neither partake in nor listen to.

"I want both of you out of this house! Now!"

The tears streamed down her cheeks as Laurel

backed from the room and ran up the stairs to change her clothes.

She closed the bedroom door behind her and fell onto a chair. It was all back. The accident. The memories of Victoria approaching her in the studio. The threats. Her hands were shaking so badly she could hardly button her blouse.

It had all been a lie. Everything she and Wade had between them was based on a lie. The reality was unbearable. She wanted to break down and pray this was just a nightmare, that she could just wake up and all would be back to normal. But she couldn't. It wasn't a nightmare; it was reality. She had to leave. She had to get out of the house before Wade came looking for her. She'd seen the pure rage in his eyes, the fury that he'd been played for a fool, and she never wanted to see that again. Nothing she could say would excuse her actions. Nor would he believe her word over that of his wife. She couldn't face him. She knew it was cowardly, but she didn't want to see the hate for her in his eyes. She could never live with that.

She quickly changed into jeans and a shirt and headed for the door. Before she walked out, she looked down at the beautiful diamond ring on her left hand. With tears blurring her vision so she was unable to focus on the brilliant diamond, she removed the ring from her finger and placed it on the nightstand. Unable to avoid one last look at the bed, where only moments before she'd lain in Wade's arms and pledged her love, she turned and ran from the room.

Once at the front door, she asked the security to summon a taxi. As soon as it arrived, she climbed in, unsure where she was going or what she was going to do. In a matter of minutes, her world had been turned upside down. And the love of her life was gone forever. As they cleared the front gates, she looked back at the mansion on the hill. Inside was the only man she would ever love. He thought she was part of Victoria's scheme to bilk him out of money by covering for her while the real Victoria disappeared to Europe to have another man's child.

Wade now would never believe she'd had amnesia or that she was forced by Victoria to live at his house. She couldn't blame Wade. He was the innocent in all of this. If what he'd told Laurel was the truth, he had fallen in love with the woman he thought her to be. He had fallen in love with his wife, which was as it should be. But now Victoria was back, and Laurel had to return to her own home and her own identity and begin again. The fairy tale was over. The magical kingdom had closed the door with her on the outside. Cinderella would return to her small world knowing she would never see her prince again.

The pain tore at her heart, threatened to overwhelm her. The tears fell like the rain outside the cab window.

She looked back one more time, but the mansion was already out of sight.

Wade Masters was beyond furious. He had been deceived by someone he trusted, someone he thought he loved. Sucker punches didn't get much worse than that. He couldn't believe it. He walked to the bar and poured himself a glass of whiskey and threw it down his throat. All this time… All this time he had played right into Victoria's hands. Unbelievable. He would never have thought she'd find a twin to help her carry out her deception. He honestly didn't know if he would ever get over this. Victoria he could deal with. She was on her way out the door as soon as she could scrape some clothes together. It was the other Victoria—Laurel— who had held his heart in her hands and crushed it.

He couldn't put all the pieces together. Yet. From what he'd gained from that quick conversation in the kitchen, the accident had started all of this. But by then, Victoria had already been on her way to the airport for the trip to Paris to have some man's baby, for God's sake. He doubted she was even sure who the father was. He expected a scam like that from Victoria, which was why he'd been about to divorce her before the accident.

But it was Laurel Dawson who'd been involved in the accident. It was Laurel, not Victoria, who woke up in the hospital not knowing who she was. Not knowing who he was. Or so she'd claimed. Victoria's plan had been diabolical. Since Wade had planned to spend the summer in London, had it not been for the accident, he would never have known. The hospital had called him because they thought his wife had been in a serious car accident. Her ID had been found in the wreckage. He'd immediately flown in from London. Flown in, come to the hospital and held a strange woman's hand while she fought to survive.

He'd known Victoria was capable of a lot of under-handed things, but this had to be her finest hour. What blew his mind was that, were it not for the accident, she would've succeeded. She would've installed a woman in his house to take her place while she did whatever she felt she had to do in Paris, and he would never have been the wiser because he was away, too.

He poured another two fingers of whiskey into his glass and drank it in one gulp. The rage was greater than anything he had ever felt. Ironically he didn't know whom to be angrier with: Victoria for setting the whole thing up; himself for walking right into it; or the woman named Laurel, who'd agreed to make the whole thing happen. That was the part that hurt the most. That was the part that wrenched his gut and left him open and bleeding.

As he began to calm down, he remembered parts of the conversation from earlier. How Laurel had tried to explain that the true story wasn't anything like the way Victoria made it sound. *That* he could believe. But what was the truth? Victoria had made a plan, Laurel had helped with it and like a total fool he'd walked right into the middle of it. Over the months they'd been to-gether, she hadn't impressed him as one who would lie and connive with no regard for the feelings of others.

Wade sat in the darkness of his home office and had another drink of the amber liquid. Victoria had returned, intending to step back into her role as his wife, with him none the wiser. She had only a month remaining of the contract that would have made her a very wealthy woman. She was just insolent enough to think she could get away with it and still receive the amount Wade was to pay her. But Wade had given her two hours to pack her bags and clear out. He'd ship what she couldn't carry with her. And he'd let his attorney take over from there. There would be no payment. She'd be damn lucky if he decided not to sue.

From a quick online search, he'd discovered that Laurel had been a free spirit, used to cutoff jeans and baggy shirts and probably going barefoot. An up-and-coming artist with great possibilities. In one picture, her dark hair was caught in a long messy braid falling over her shoulder as she smiled her beautiful smile at the camera.

But it didn't matter. Hell, it didn't matter at all. Victoria had been caught. Laurel Dawson had been forced to come clean regarding her role in the scheme, and he had learned a very valuable lesson: don't trust anyone. Ever.

Wade had seen the hurt and remorse in her eyes for only a few seconds before Laurel had run past him and out the door into the night. How could she have betrayed him like that?

The rain continued to fall outside, lending its sweet smell to the foul odor of deception he sensed throughout the house. And as if on cue, Victoria walked past him just then with absolute audacity, as though she was the one wronged in all of this.

"Get all your things and get out," Wade couldn't resist saying. "And don't forget the painting in the library. I want no reminder of your presence in this house. Needless to say, you just relinquished any claim to any money you might otherwise have had."

"We'll see about that when my attorneys get finished reviewing this mess. And that's not my painting in your library. It came from the little bitch. She painted it. I bought it two days before she convinced me that her plan would work and encouraged me to go to Paris, assuring me everything would be fine."

Wade knew that was a lie. But he didn't see any reason to drag it out further by arguing. "It doesn't make any difference. You lost at any rate. But I would like to know one thing. How did you find her? How did you find someone that looks so much like you?"

Victoria's body slumped forward as though she had maintained an air of false indignity as long as she could. "My older sister had a baby out of wedlock and had to give her up. My curiosity got the better of me, and I tracked her down. As soon as I saw her… Wade, I made a mistake, and I had to go to Paris to make it right. I might have been wrong in not coming clean with you up front, but, after all the verbal attacks and warnings to keep my affairs discreet, I didn't really know how you would react to a pregnancy."

"What happened to the baby?"

"I left her with friends in Paris. I will be joining them as soon as things are arranged over here. I plan to start adoption proceedings when I bring her back. For what it's worth, this was not an attempt to purposely defy or shame you in any way."

"You just wanted the million dollars."

"Yes."

"Victoria, you are a piece of work." She'd been only a month out from their contract ending. But by then her baby would have been born and clearly he wanted no part of that. It was between Victoria and the father of the child. Bad timing on her part, to say the least.

He took three seconds to let his eyes roam across the face of this despicable woman before he turned and walked out of the room.

Victoria would soon be forever gone from this house, never to return. He wouldn't listen to one syllable of her whining or her lies. And Laurel was gone as well.

Which was fine with him, too.

Thirteen

"It's almost five o'clock," Beth Hamilton called from the back of the small shop. "I think we can start to clean up for the day."

Beth's store in the small town of Waxahachie was a combination art gallery and learning center for the neighborhood. Some twenty students from finger-painting five-year-olds to the more versatile teenagers and young adults filled the art studio on a daily basis and after school for their group and one-on-one instruction in painting with watercolors and acrylics. A couple of the older kids and adults had begun using oils, and it reminded Laurel of her own excitement when she'd first worked with that medium many years ago.

It didn't take Laurel long to clean the already cleaned work spaces and tidy up in preparation for the next day.

"How are you coming on your painting?" Beth asked as she came into the back studio. "Are you gonna let me see this one?"

Laurel shrugged. "I don't know why you make such a big deal of my paintings. They are just landscapes, nothing new about them."

Beth walked over to an easel standing in the corner. Carefully removing the drop cloth, she stood back and contemplated the canvas before her.

"This is amazing. Even better than the last few, and that's saying something." She replaced the cover on the canvas. "You know, Mrs. Bridgeman is going to have a hissy fit if you don't let her put your collection in one of her gallery exhibits."

"I don't have a collection," Laurel corrected. "And these are not for a showing."

"Seriously, Laurel. You know you are an exceptional artist. I wish you would let her show them just one time and see what happens." Beth shook her head. "I can't imagine where you come up with the landscapes that you do. I'm pretty sure the places don't exist anywhere on this planet."

Laurel smiled but said nothing. The images to which Beth referred were not in Laurel's imagination. They were in her memory, indelibly permanent, but for her eyes only. They were the special places she'd gone with Wade. The pine forest, the still pool, the small waterfall, the pastures with the cattle and calves and the horses whose spirit shone in their eyes. These memories were her life now. She would never see them again. But, somehow, with each brushstroke she felt close to Wade: his deep voice, his warm breath against her skin, his brooding laughter. It was all she had. She didn't want to share them with anyone, let alone put them on public display. That would be wrong. It would be sharing personal, precious moments with the world. They were her memories. They were all she had left of the man she'd loved and still loved.

It had taken over a month before she could pick up the ruins of her life and trudge forward again. She'd stayed with Beth for a while, withdrawn and silent. Beth had picked up on something not right and hadn't pushed her for any answers. Gradually, Laurel had begun to try to rejoin the world of the living. At first, she'd refused to go out with their other friends, preferring to stay at home, quietly remembering, silently crying with a broken heart she knew would never heal. But eventually she'd joined their small group of six old and loyal friends, who didn't push her for information but were just grateful she was taking a few first steps. They knew something horrendous had happened during the months she'd been gone. And clearly they could see that it had broken her soul. Laurel appreciated their friendship and understanding, and it was that understanding that had eventually brought her around.

Her oldest friend, Beth, had done the most. Finally, unable to listen to another night of sobs from her guest room, she had given Laurel a good shake, figuratively, and demanded to know what had happened. To be fair, Laurel told her some of the story. Very little, however.

Just that she'd met the wrong man and had become heartbroken through her foolishness. Relieved that Laurel wasn't suffering some debilitating disease, Beth had finally left her alone to work through the shredded emotions. She gave her a place to tuck her tail and hide from the world and provided friendship and encouragement when it was needed.

"Mrs. Bridgeman will not give up," Beth persisted. "She has been a fan of your work since we were in high school, and she will have that showing. Are you staying over tonight?"

"Yeah. I'd like to work here for a while, if that's okay?"

"Of course. Just be sure to grab a bite to eat. There's some fruit and some lunch meat in the fridge. If you lose any more weight… Just eat, okay?"

"Okay."

She heard Beth tidying the front of the small art studio and the clang of the cash register as her friend put the day's take in a bank bag. Then, after a friendly *See ya tomorrow!* there was the tinkle of the bell over the door, and all was quiet.

Laurel walked to the corner of the room where her current work in progress was propped on its easel and took the cover off. It was another one of the old hunters' cabin from a different angle. The use of alternating shadow and light made each tile of the roof stand out. The overall impression was one of gentle decay. The painting was set in the fall, and leaves fell dispassionately down over the entire scene, the reds, golds, greens

and browns swirling around the old chimney and ac-
cumulating on the ground. Rays of sun broke through
the clouds, highlighting the hundred-and-fifty-year-
old structure. Maybe that was why she was drawn to
it. So many things in her life never lasted. Her mother
had died when she was born and, with no other rela-
tives, Laurel had had a firsthand glimpse of the state's
foster-care system. Going from family to family, house
to house, she had always felt like she was on the brink
of losing it all.

But she'd always had art. It was the one thing that
got her through the hard times. A small sketch pad and
a pencil had become her best friends. Inside the pages
of her spiral notebooks were images of the people and
places that, when compiled, told her story. Good, bad or
indifferent, she'd captured the visuals and the essence
that made up her life.

The tolling of midnight from the bell tower of the
small church across the street brought her back into
the here and now. Stretching, she flexed her back and
dropped the brushes into the cleaning solution. She sat
back rubbing her neck and looked at the picture in front
of her. Better. Some of the details could be enhanced,
but for the most part she was happy with her work.
Through the smell of turpentine she could almost sense
the tang of fall in the air that surrounded the little cabin.
Thanks to Wade, there would be plenty more pictures
to paint. It was the only release from her tortured mind.
Images of Wade caught unawares by something she'd
said or done. Or rubbing the bump on his head with a

towel after he'd upended the table in the middle of the hallway. And the incurably adorable look on his face in the moments of discovery of anything he should have already known.

What she could neither paint nor forget was the look on his face the last time they'd ever made eye contact. The waves of fury at having been played for a fool. The look that said *I trusted you. How could you do this to me?* The internal rage that distorted his handsome features into a mosaic of the raw pain of betrayal.

She carefully replaced the protective cover over the canvas, rinsed and dried her brushes, and turned off the light on her way out. Tomorrow was Sunday, the one day of the week she dreaded. No kids came on Sunday. The little bell over the door didn't ring. No shoppers filled the still time. Beth wasn't there, telling her what she had to eat for lunch. It was a day to remember. A day to try to forget. One more day to somehow get through. A sixteen-hour day applying paint to canvas, bringing alive memories both bitter and sweet. It was a day to live inside the vacuum, where pain could only get in if she wasn't strong enough to prevent it. She had to prevail. If not, the feelings would intrude and yet again shatter the bruised remnants of her heart.

Wade had ensured Victoria made it out of his house and off his property, and he let his security staff and attorneys handle the rest. Clearly, going to Paris or anywhere else to have another man's child broke the stipulations of their contract. But dammed if she hadn't almost gotten away with it. For all Victoria knew, Wade had been in London during the months she was away and Laurel was taking her place. The whole scenario was intended to play out with him none the wiser. ·

Then an eighteen-wheeler had run a red light.

And when he thought of Laurel, all that surfaced was the look on her face when he'd screamed at both women to get out. Laurel had run from the room, and he'd not spoken to her again since then.

It had been over a month, and Wade still couldn't let go. His instincts told him to walk away from it all. Be glad he was rid of both of them. His heart said he should go to her. She'd been played as much as he had. Laurel was the first and only woman he'd ever loved. He honestly believed she loved him, too. Or had, before he'd lost his temper big-time the night Victoria had come wandering home. Would Laurel still want anything to do with him after he'd lost it and screamed for them both to get out of his house?

He'd found her ring on the nightstand. His heart had lurched when he picked it up. She could have gotten a pretty penny for it. The fact that she left it behind said something. Didn't it?

He ran both hands through his hair. Victoria had admitted that Laurel had refused to take any money. Was she, in fact, the pawn in Victoria's scheme? Had it been her fault the car was hit by a truck? Had she faked amnesia? No. He couldn't believe any of that. No one was that good of an actress. She had loved the ranch, the horses, swimming in the mountain pool. All of the things that meant most to him Laurel loved as well. Deep down, Wade knew he would never find another woman who was so incredibly perfect for him. But could he find her? And if he did, would it be wasted effort? Would she even speak to him again after the hateful way he'd treated her in the end?

He reached over and picked up the house phone and dialed the number to his security division. "Matt? I need you to find someone, if you can. As soon as possible."

Laurel was so angry at Beth she wanted to hit something. There had been plenty of times she'd said *yes* to an exhibit of her paintings, but showing those of Wade and the ranch was a big fat loud *no*. Beth had gone behind her back and done it anyway, arranging it with Mrs. Bridgeman. And it wasn't as if they were going to be shown in a small exhibit hall. Oh no, they were, at this moment, on their way to Dallas. She needed to get to the art gallery and see if she could protect her privacy and prevent this from happening.

Even though it was only three o'clock in the afternoon, she closed the shop early, flipping the sign from Open to Closed, and hurried to her car. It was a good hour's drive from Waxahachie to Dallas if she didn't run into the ever-present road construction. Backing out of the parking space, she put the car in Drive and headed south.

It was almost five when she turned into the parking lot of the art gallery. She noted Beth's car parked next to the building.

"What do you think?" Beth asked when Laurel finally entered. "Great place, huh?"

"Where are they?"

"In the back. Oh, come on, Laurel, don't be mad. This is what you've worked for your entire life."

"Not with these paintings. Beth, you don't understand. I thought you did."

"Come on. There are some from before your accident and a couple since. They gave you two entire walls. I think it looks spectacular."

Laurel rounded the far corner, and there they were. Still lifes, landscapes, portraits. The one of the woman sitting on a stone wall holding a rose against the backdrop of a sunset was still one of her favorites. Then, on another part of the wall, there were the landscapes of the ranch. All served to bring the walls to life.

"How long?" Laurel asked Beth.

"The showing is just for the weekend. Well, Friday, Saturday and Sunday."

There were seven of Laurel's paintings in all. Among the landscapes were smaller, individual canvases focused on smaller things. Like the pinecone hanging from a tree branch, the early-morning dew making it look fresh and crisp.

"That one is adorable." Beth pointed at the calf with its mother. "And I love the mystery men." She turned to Laurel, grabbed her arm and spun her around. In front of her were two portraits.

Laurel's heart dropped to her knees as she stared at the two portraits of Wade Masters. She hadn't noticed when she was painting them, but Wade was every man; the stern, cold, brooding man of wealth and privilege. Used to commanding a boardroom and governing financial aspects of international corporations, he was a powerful man who expected to be treated to lavish parties and approached about supporting governors and top politicians. The second painting was of a man who was carefree, had no worries other than concerns of family and close friends. This was a guy in worn jeans and an open shirt and whose hair was tousled by the wind. One who would jump on a motorcycle and do wheelies in the dirt, who would throw a saddle on a horse and cut cows for fifteen hours straight. One who was content with who he was and the world around him. A man who judged others by their actions and their word. It was this man Laurel had fallen in love with. It was this man she had hurt.

"Laurel, is that him?"

She could only stare, and a trickle of fear ran through her. If Wade found out about this viewing, he would truly and thoroughly hate her. That being said, he already did. What did she have to lose if he found out? They were, after all, her paintings. Maybe she owed it to the world to let people see what a complex, brilliant and loving man Wade Masters was.

"Yeah."

"Which one?"

She looked back and forth between the two paintings. "Both."

* * *

Wade had never seen anything like it. A complete section of the Montrella Art Gallery contained pictures of his home. Detailed paintings of the lower falls and swimming holes, the valleys and the pine groves. Insightful, detailed glimpses of his ranch, captured forever. There was one of the old trappers' cabin, next to the spring and Stockman's Ridge with the view of the valley spread out far below.

When he'd first been told that paintings by a new artist were to be included in an exhibit of another artist's work, he'd look at Sylvia Fields, his senior administrative assistant, like she had grown a second head.

"Do I look like an art connoisseur? Why would I care?"

"Because two of the paintings are of you and I'm guessing the landscapes are of your ranch."

Laurel had done this. Her skills, perspective and amazing talent had brought the ranch alive. His mother was considered a great artist, but nothing near this scale. He slowly walked the area, looking at each picture, seeing his valley through her eyes. There was great beauty in each scene, even in the painting of the old hunters' cabin. But it was as he turned the last corner he saw the portraits of himself.

To say he was stunned would be an understatement. There were two paintings. One was the facade he showed to the world; the other revealed the side he kept hidden from all but close friends and family. Laurel had nailed each one perfectly. She had seen through the mask and knew both men intimately.

Only someone who saw the differences in his character, who knew him that well, could have painted his portrait so authentically. She'd painted what she saw. First the cowboy who enjoyed letting his hair down and eating beans around a campfire. Then the hard, cynical businessman he became in Dallas.

"Mr. Masters." The woman he'd asked about speaking to the artist returned, wringing her hands. Never a good sign. "I'm so sorry, but she just left. I couldn't find anyone who knew when she would be back. But I can tell you the paintings are not for sale. There was a misunderstanding between the owner of the art gallery, Mrs. Bridgeman, and the artist. These were not intended to be shown. May I give Ms. Dawson a message or a phone number?"

Wade shook his head. "She knows how to reach me. Consider each and every one of these paintings sold. I don't care what you were told. If Mrs. Bridgeman has a problem with that, she can work it out with my accountant. You will receive a call in a few minutes from Bradley Jarrod, who will arrange for payment and delivery." He glanced once again at the paintings. "I stress, Mrs. Colbert," he said, reading her name tag, "do not let one single painting by this artist leave the building other than under my instructions."

"Of course, sir," she assured him, a light of excitement appearing in her eyes. "In fact, we'll close the section so no one else can see them."

"Good." Wade turned and headed for the door, Crawford and Jenkins flanking him. They drew glances from others as they walked toward the front door, but Wade ignored it. He had more on his mind than dim-witted people who might be staring. Laurel had been here. The gallery attendant had indicated she'd left only moments before he arrived. If she knew he was here, she'd managed to slip by him. It wouldn't happen again.

"Laurel," said Beth over the phone. "Your paintings… they sold. All of them."

"Sold?" It couldn't be. She hadn't intended for them to be shown, let alone sold.

"You and Mrs. Bridgeman can't do that. I told you not to—"

"I think it's okay," Beth broke in. "They were all sold to one man. I wasn't there, but I'm betting it was Wade Masters. That's who's in the portraits, isn't it, Laurel?"

Laurel didn't respond.

"Yeah, I thought so. Anyway, thought I'd give you a heads-up. He asked for you and didn't look happy when he was told you weren't here. He and the two men with him, I'm guessing bodyguards, walked out after he'd arranged to buy the paintings. I'll bet they are headed your way."

"He doesn't know where I live."

"Don't be dumb. If he found the paintings, he can find you. You love him. I'm guessing he loves you, too. If he isn't there in an hour, you can say I was wrong and throw it in my face the rest of my life. But you need to talk with him, Laurel. Whatever happened between you needs to be worked out."

The line went dead.

What had happened at the Masters estate wasn't something that could be worked out or made better. She had ensconced herself in another woman's house, assumed her identity and made love with her husband. In fact, she'd fallen in love with her husband. It was all immoral, possibly even illegal. She knew he was hurt. And angry. Put in his position she would be livid.

She was certain he'd heard about the art showing and had gone there to correct a foolish mistake. He'd probably felt required to purchase the paintings to keep his privacy intact. She knew if Wade found out about the exhibit, he would be angry. She should have demanded the paintings be taken down instead of just saying they were not for sale. She just hadn't expected him to find them so soon.

Regardless of how much he must hate her, Laurel didn't regret a second of their time together. She still loved Wade deeply. It wasn't supposed to have happened this way. She should never have met him, let alone had the chance to fall in love with him. And now he thought her a woman as conniving and malevolent as his wife. No doubt he thought she was trying to make money off the paintings of his beloved ranch. Laurel blinked back the tears and gritted her teeth to combat the surge of pain again slashing her heart. Were Wade and Victoria back together? Was Wade holding her in his arms even now? Making love to her? Ironically, all Laurel would ever have of the man she loved were a few precious memories.

She headed into the back room of the paint school, where her current painting was still under wraps. The feel of adding paint to a canvas always helped to soothe her nerves and prevent her mind from wandering to places she didn't want to go.

But knowing Wade had walked into the art exhibit in Dallas and seen her paintings brought that last night back to the forefront of her mind. The sheer horror of it all. It seemed no matter how hard she tried, she just couldn't seem to get it right. First agreeing to Victoria's scheme, then allowing an opportunity for Beth and Mrs. Bridgeman to waylay her paintings and take them to an exhibition. And Wade had walked into the middle both times.

She selected two brushes and uncovered the canvas. Turning on the extra lights, she scrutinized the painting. Artificial lighting was different from true sunlight. She would have to be careful, but she couldn't bear to go home. She would just wind up back here after pacing the floor half the night.

"That's very interesting."

Spinning around, she faced Wade.

Even backlit, he could tell she had gone pale. He watched her closely, afraid she would again disappear. The painting she'd been working on was going home with him, and it would remain there until he could figure out what had happened to the brilliant artist whose technique had changed so drastically. He'd fallen in love with the artist who had painted it. And more than anything wanted her back in his life.

"How did you get in here?" she asked, her eyes darting around the room as though looking for a way out. The art room had only one door, and Wade was standing in front of it.

He held up a key. "Thanks to Beth Hamilton." He tossed the key onto the table. "I was wrong, Laurel. That night. When I told you to go. I was speaking through anger and frustration, and I didn't mean to direct it at you."

"Yes, you did. I saw your face." She began to back up and ease around the large table at the center of the room. "You have every right to hate me. I didn't know what I was doing at the time, but if I hadn't been in the wreck, I still would have been at your house. I would still have pretended to be Victoria."

"Because she threatened you if you didn't," he countered and took a step forward. "She came clean about those threats. If the only thing I had in this world was threatened, I would probably give in, too."

"No, you wouldn't. You're strong. You're a fighter. I'm not."

"You're the strongest woman I know. You are the most honest person I've ever met. And I love you, Laurel Dawson."

She bowed her head, giving it a slight shake, and the tears began to roll down her face.

"Look at me, Laurel."

She shook her head. "No."

Then she felt his hand under her chin, slowly raising her face to his. Her lilac eyes glimmered from unshed tears, making them appear almost iridescent. "I think you love me, too."

She sniffed, unable to confirm what he said for fear it was a ploy.

"So, what are we going to do about this?"

When she didn't respond, he stepped closer to her and placed his other hand against her face. "Victoria is gone, never to return. Our divorce was final last week. I want you to come home with me. I want us to be as we were before that fateful night. Only this time, you know who you are. You have your memories. I fell in love with you a long time ago. I just mistakenly called you by a different name. Marry me, Laurel Marie Dawson."

He lowered his face to her, giving her the option of kissing him. With a small whimper, she placed her hand against his chest, and her lips against his. It was as though time had never interfered; they were back living and loving as they had been before. Her lips were hungry, and he was ready and more than willing to fill that hunger.

"Marry me," he whispered against her lips.

"Yes—"

She barely had the word out before he pulled her hard against him and kissed her deeply, passionately. "I love you so much." Then he was kissing her again, his body reacting as it had always done to this beautiful woman.

"The paintings." She broke the kiss. "I didn't intend for them to be shown. They were only for me. Beth…"

"It's okay, sweetheart," he said. "They are coming home with us. They're beautiful, and I will enjoy looking at them the rest of my life. Someday we may even decide to share them with the world."

Then he took her left hand and pulled the diamond ring from his pocket and slipped it on her finger. "We will be married tomorrow. I refuse to wait one second longer. Later, if you want a big wedding celebration, you can have whatever you wish. But I don't intend to wait another full day without knowing legally, spiritually, emotionally—in every way that matters—you are mine."

Tears filled her eyes as he again pulled her into his arms, held tight in his embrace. His mouth covered hers, and their love soared.

Epilogue

The wedding was held in a small country church on the ranch. Old and forgotten for years, the building had been refurbished, painted and filled with new pews and the restored altar. White roses and mums with matching white ribbons decorated the interior, spilling out into the trees surrounding the church.

Wade's brothers and their wives were there, along with the ranch hands and a few special friends. It was a family wedding. That was what Laurel wanted, so that was what Wade had provided.

Although they had been officially married for a couple of months, Laurel had wanted a ceremony that could be shared by their closest friends and family. She arrived at the church in a barouche pulled by two white horses, their harness adorned with matching white roses and ribbons. Wade was waiting at the entrance and helped her from the carriage.

After the ceremony, the party lasted for hours, held in the covered pavilion a mile from the main house. Country music filled the air, and the summer night set the stage for a wonderful evening. "Are you ready to sneak out of here?" Wade asked his bride as they danced. "I need to get you home." He pulled her close, and she felt his erection against her belly.

"I'll follow you," she replied, smiling. She wanted to be alone with her husband and knew the night ahead would be magical. It was always so when she was in his arms.

Wade took her hand, and she marveled again at how strong and warm he was as he led her the few steps to the front door. His car was parked right outside.

"I love you, Laurel Masters."

She smiled as he started the car and followed the path to the main ranch area, then on to Pine House. When they got there, he helped her from the car, then picked her up in his arms and carried her up the steps and inside the front door. Not pausing there, he went up the stairs and into the master suite.

Setting her down, he lost no time removing the beautiful silk gown and the diamond-encrusted pin that held her hair, cascading slowly past her shoulders.

Laurel removed his silk shirt and bow tie and pulled at his belt, unzipping his pants. Wade kicked out of his pants, cupped her face with his big hands and brought his mouth down over hers. Laurel was lost. She fell deep into his arms and kissed him back with all the love she felt for this great man.

He turned the lights out and lifted her into the bed.

"I'm going to love you forever," he said against her mouth, his voice deep and rough.

"As I will you," Laurel replied and pulled his head down to hers.

And neither spoke another word for a very long time.

* * * * *

*Can't get enough of
The Masters of Texas?*

*Don't miss Seth Masters's story
available January 2019
from Lauren Canan
and Harlequin Desire.*

*If you're on Twitter, tell us what you
think of Harlequin Desire! #harlequindesire*

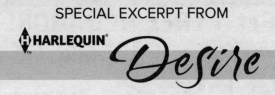
Benjamin Bennett was a catch by anyone's standards—
even before you factored in his healthy bank account.
But he was her best friend's little brother. And though he
was all grown-up now, he was just a kid compared to her.

Flirting with Benji would start tongues wagging all
over Magnolia Lake. Not that she cared what they thought
of her. But if the whole town started talking, it would
make things uncomfortable for the people she loved.

"Thanks for the dance."

Benji lowered their joined hands but didn't let go.
Instead, he leaned down, his lips brushing her ear and his
well-trimmed beard gently scraping her neck. "Let's get
out of here."

It was a bad idea. A really bad idea.

Her cheeks burned. "But it's your cousin's wedding."

He nodded toward Blake, who was dancing with his

bride, Savannah, as their infant son slept on his shoulder. The man was in complete bliss.

"I doubt he'll notice I'm gone. Besides, you'd be rescuing me. If Jeb Dawson tells me one more time about his latest invention—"

"Okay, okay." Sloane held back a giggle as she glanced around the room. "You need to escape as badly as I do. But there's no way we're leaving here together. It'd be on the front page of the newspaper by morning."

"Valid point." Benji chuckled. "So meet me at the cabin."

"The cabin on the lake?" She had so many great memories of weekends spent there.

It would just be two old friends catching up on each other's lives. Nothing wrong with that.

She repeated it three times in her head. But there was nothing friendly about the sensations that danced along her spine when he'd held her in his arms and pinned her with that piercing gaze.

"Okay. Maybe we can catch up over a cup of coffee or something."

"Or something." The corner of his sensuous mouth curved in a smirk.

A shiver ran through her as she wondered, for the briefest moment, how his lips would taste.

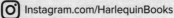